WITHOUT VANITY OR PRIDE

A PRIDE AND PREJUDICE VARIATION DUOLOGY

L M ROMANO
AMY D'ORAZIO

Quills & Quartos
PUBLISHING

Edited by Julie Cooper and Debbie Styne

Cover by Evelyne Labelle, Carpe Librum Book Design

ISBN 978-1-963213-13-3 (ebook) and 978-1-963213-14-0 (paperback)

CONTENTS

NO IMPROPER PRIDE
Amy D'Orazio

INSUFFICIENT VANITY
LM Romano

NO IMPROPER PRIDE

AMY D'ORAZIO

"I love him. Indeed he has no improper pride. He is perfectly amiable. You do not know what he really is; then pray do not pain me by speaking of him in such terms."

— ELIZABETH BENNET, PRIDE & PREJUDICE CHAPTER 39

CHAPTER ONE

May 1812, Hyde Park

Though it was not quite the fashionable hour, the paths through Hyde Park were crowded, the populace of London seemingly uniformly determined to take advantage of the fine spring sunshine. The rains of spring had begun to abate, and Fitzwilliam Darcy hoped, rather than believed, the ache in his heart would soon do likewise.

It had been nearly a month since Elizabeth Bennet's scathing rejection of his offer of marriage. The first week had been marked by shocked fury as he contemplated, endlessly, the terrible accusations she had hurled at him. The second week, fury had dissipated as he had recognised, reluctantly, the justice in *some* of what she had said. The third week, despair set in as he recognised she

5

was *entirely* correct. He had been selfish, disdainful, conceited, arrogant, and he was wholly unworthy of her.

In the last week, the fourth since that fateful night at Hunsford parsonage, he was resolved to forget her. What else could he do? He could not loll about like a maudlin schoolgirl, no matter that he felt quite maudlin. *Keep busy,* he told himself, *outrun the agony.* So it was that he forced himself into intense occupation nearly every minute of the day, scarcely allowing himself a moment's rest until he dropped into his bed, exhausted, at night. It had been, thus far, mostly unsuccessful, but he reasoned if he just kept at it, he would conquer his feelings.

"Come walk in the park with me," he said to Viscount Saye, nearly the second his cousin entered his study.

Saye ignored him and walked over to the bookshelf. "You own *Thérèse the Philosopher,* yes?"

"I do not. A walk? Will you join me?"

"I am positive you must." Saye looked over his shoulder from his perusal of Darcy's shelves. "I was with Sir Frederick this morning at our club, and Mr George Boyer comes by and tells us that the author was his great grandmother—"

"The author was a man."

"The protagonist then," Saye replied impatiently. "So Boyer rattles on some nonsense about the truth in it, and he and Fred begin to argue over it, so I told Fred,

'Why not see if what he says is true? Darcy is sure to own it'."

"Alas, I do not," Darcy replied. "I am not in the habit of filling my family library with erotica."

"Yet, you clearly know the story, else you should not have known it was erotica," Saye replied with a smirk.

Darcy rolled his eyes, ignoring the gibe. "Come with me to the park."

Saye could not go easily. He insisted on looking over all the shelves, heedless of the system of organisation that Darcy employed; he then concluded the tome must be at Pemberley; and lastly, he decried walking as a hopelessly common endeavour and suggested they ride. Darcy waited patiently while his cousin rattled away, secretly rejoicing in the effortless expenditure of time, and at length the two gentlemen set out.

"I have never known you to be in such a fever to promenade during the fashionable hour," Saye remarked as they went. "Dare I say you are prepared to find another lady to woo?"

In an unguarded moment a se'nnight past—one on the end of a difficult day in which too much brandy and too little food had been consumed—Darcy had confessed all to Saye. His cousin had been particularly vexatious all day long, teasing him about being a gloomy miss and wondering aloud and loudly whether Darcy's courses were plaguing him. At length, Darcy could take no more and begged him to leave off.

But Saye would not leave off, not until he was in possession of every mortifying morsel.

To his credit, knowing the truth of the matter made him desist. Alas, Darcy found this to be even worse, having become an object of pity for a man widely known to be merciless.

"She must be an idiot," Saye had opined, with a clap on his younger cousin's back. "She could have been married to one of the wealthiest men in England!"

"She is *not* an idiot," Darcy had replied quietly. "I am."

In the week since, Saye had contrived a number of remedies for Darcy's spirits, including cock fights, a race with the Four-in-Hand Club, cards, and now, ladies. Darcy considered telling Saye that no, he absolutely was not prepared to consider making love to another woman; however, as they entered the park, Saye's head swivelled about madly, taking in the many ladies and gentlemen moving about. As it seemed to be occupying him nicely, Darcy did not protest.

"She is a fine-looking—no, no, too fair. That is, unless you seek a fair-haired lady this time?"

"I do not want anyone at all, save for her."

"Miss Bennet was…?"

"Her hair is dark."

"Darker or lighter than your own?"

"What does it matter? Darker," Darcy replied impatiently.

"I wonder if she possesses some sort of Gypsy blood? Or Italian! Those Italians can certainly dress a person down. Now, there!" Saye made a gesture with his hand. "What say you to that charming creature just that way?"

"That *charming creature* looks like she is Georgiana's age."

"What about that one?" Saye gestured again.

Darcy shook his head. "Pray stop. There is no use to any of this."

But Saye would persist until Darcy's head ached, and he was seriously considering shoving his cousin into the Serpentine. Fortunately, they paused a moment as Saye's present love interest, Miss Lillian Goddard, peeped at him from within a cluster of young ladies some distance away. He tipped his hat, which made some of her friends giggle, though Miss Goddard was sedate and only nodded in reply.

"Nothing like a sweet-looking blonde in my opinion," Saye mused happily. "Miss Goddard has a sister you know, and just as pretty as she is."

"Also lately married."

"Lord Jermyn? The man is half dead already. We will all be dancing at his funeral, likely before you are done moping over Miss Bennet."

With a roll of his eyes, Darcy enquired, "Why on earth would we dance at his funer—"

His voice died, for when he raised his eyes, he saw her. His heart dropped into his Hessians at the sight.

He knew it had been a dreadful idea to come to the park. At the fashionable hour no less! Idiot! But the day was nearly sublime, and even he had grown weary of sulking in his library. He would pay dearly for this fit of good humour.

"What is it?" Saye asked.

"Shh. I mean, stop. Slower."

"You wish me to walk slower?"

She had not as yet seen them. She, Miss Bennet, and another lady unknown to him had paused to examine some plant by the side of the path. Having satisfied whatever curiosity they possessed regarding it, the ladies turned and began to walk again.

"Walk slower? Or talk slower?" Saye asked again.

Darcy gave the sleeve of his cousin's coat an impatient tug. "Walk slower, or let us linger here a minute or two. We cannot...that is to say, I do not wish to...I see some...people...a person...it would be for the best if we did not meet one another."

With a profound and humiliating lack of discretion, Saye began to crane his neck, asking loudly about this person or that, and why Darcy would not like to meet them.

"Pray lower your voice," Darcy hissed through gritted teeth. "It is her."

He gestured with one finger to where the trio of interest walked ahead of them on the path.

"Her?" Saye widened his eyes and dropped his jaw to

a comically wide degree. In a whisper-shout, he asked, "Miss Elizabeth Bennet? Here?"

"If you will only join me in hanging back a bit, I do not doubt they may divert to another path soon, or perhaps stop to speak to someone, and then we shall—"

Saye turned to him, eyes alit with anticipation. He gave Darcy a little tap on the chest. "I want to meet her."

"Absolutely not. We must avoid her notice at all costs."

"Avoid her notice? I could not think of it. Indeed, I must be acquainted with this magical creature." Saye rubbed his hands together delightedly. "Which is she? My money is on the one in green."

"Half the park is wearing green, and I refuse to introduce you."

"Dark hair, curls at the nape, straw bonnet, Pomona green pelisse." Saye lifted one brow in triumph. "I see by your face that I am correct."

"Nevertheless, we are not meeting them."

"Why not?"

Darcy sighed. "You know why not. She wishes to speak to me as little as I would like to speak to her."

"Ah! But I daresay you *would* like to speak to her, so that assertion is sheer puffery."

Saye had him on that point. Against everything, Darcy *did* want to speak to her, even if it would be awkward and painful and dissatisfying. Even if Elizabeth wished to upbraid him again, he would endure it for the sheer enjoyment of the time spent in her presence.

"I would not impose myself upon her. I am certain it could only bring pain to us both."

Saye had stopped in the middle of the path and regarded the ladies with a cocked head and one hand on his hip. "Perhaps not. Perhaps she would like to see you again."

Darcy chuckled bitterly. "Indeed, I am very certain she does not."

"How do you know? What did she say after she read your letter? What did she think of it?"

"After the letter?" The ladies had moved from the path and were making their way towards the bank of the Serpentine. His eyes followed their progress. "I do not know."

"What do you mean you do not know? You handed her the letter, she opened it to read it, and then…?"

"I handed her the letter, and then I left her. I did not stay to see if she read it, nor can I imagine what she thought of it." He swallowed, watching as Elizabeth, Miss Bennet, and the other lady joined a group of two small girls and what appeared to be a governess or nursemaid. "She might have thrown it directly into the fire for all I know."

"I do not think so. She looks like the curious sort."

"It occurs to me now that the letter was written in a

dreadful bitterness of spirit. I am ashamed of what I said."

"Whatever you wrote regarding Wickham could not be said with sufficient vitriol."

Darcy nodded. "Yes, but the other things about...her family and—well, I am wholly persuaded that there is every possibility that the letter only angered her more."

Saye turned his scrutiny from the ladies to Darcy and screwed up his face in a parody of bewilderment. "You insulted her family verbally—which may have been forgiven as we are all intemperate when angry—but then repeated the offences in *writing?*"

"Yes, and as I have told you repeatedly, I am ashamed of my conduct and certain she despises me for it. So we certainly should not plague her with my presence here."

"How very like you that is!"

"To wish not to pain her?"

"To have the last word," Saye retorted. "You must have the last word in any argument, and that is exactly what you have done to Miss Elizabeth Bennet—handed her a packet full of insults and then ran off before she could reply."

"I did not run off."

"Neither did you allow her to respond. Should she not have been permitted to have her say?"

"I assure you," said Darcy, "she said quite enough."

"She likely thought you had said quite enough as

well, yet she paid you the compliment of hearing—or rather reading—your final words on the matter."

"We do not know what she did with my final words," Darcy reminded him.

"I think this Miss Elizabeth Bennet deserves her chance to give you a final proper set-down too."

"My letter was not meant to be a set-down, it was merely—"

"You just said you wrote it in a dreadful bitterness of spirit!"

"I did but...well, yes."

"So perhaps she too deserves the opportunity to unburden herself of whatever bitterness of spirit *she* may possess."

"Let me understand you. You wish me to approach a lady, in full view of her sister and friends and nearly every person of fashion in this park, and give her the opportunity to upbraid me?"

"And maybe once she has," Saye teased him with a grin and shake of his finger, "just maybe she might then be willing to entertain the notion of giving you another chance to woo her."

"Impossible," Darcy scoffed.

"It certainly will be impossible if all you ever do is skulk along behind her, avoiding her notice." Saye punched his arm. "I am going over there."

"You do not know them!" Darcy cried to Saye's departing back.

"I shall introduce myself."

"You cannot! Every rule of polite society forbids it!"

Saye turned and grinned lazily, walking backwards with his eyes on Darcy. "Why should I care two straws for that? I am rich, devilishly handsome, and titled. I make my own rules. Now, either you come along and introduce me or I introduce myself, and she will know your relations are as abominably rude as you are."

By some mystical inducement, Darcy felt his feet begin to move. "She already knows my relations are nothing to boast of," he muttered. "She has met Lady Catherine."

CHAPTER TWO

E lizabeth thought that she and Jane must surely be a burden to bear for their dear aunt. Although Mrs Gardiner showed no sign of wearying of them, between Jane's dispirited languor and her own peevish doldrums, they were not fit to be in company. Elizabeth tried to be a better houseguest, but she continued to find herself sinking into self-recrimination for how she had behaved.

I meant to be uncommonly clever in taking so decided a dislike to him without any reason. It is such a spur to one's genius, such an opening for wit, to have a dislike of that kind. One may be continually abusive without saying anything just, but one cannot be always laughing at a man without now and then stumbling on something witty.

Fortunately, Mrs Gardiner was a determined hostess and refused to allow her nieces to persist in their melancholy, even if in Elizabeth's case, she did not understand the reasons for it. *Likely, she thinks it mere sisterly affection,* Elizabeth surmised. She had considered taking her sister and aunt into her confidence but could not do it. She had made herself ridiculous with her prejudice against Mr Darcy, driven by vanity to be pleased by a villain, and to scorn the truly decent gentleman. She knew it and disliked her conduct well enough; she could not bear the weight of Jane's or her aunt Gardiner's censure on top of it.

After a long morning of sighs and snappish witticisms, Mrs Gardiner asked, "What say you to a trip to Hyde Park?"

Their young cousins, Elspeth and Millie, were immediately delighted by the scheme and ran off to retrieve their little bonnets and wraps. The plans were settled before either Jane or Elizabeth had uttered yea or nay, but it was of no consequence. *The fresh air will do us good,* Elizabeth decided.

The task of getting six ladies—Jane, Elizabeth, Mrs Gardiner, the two Miss Gardiners and their governess, Miss Franklin—the short distance to the park was not an inconsiderable one. But the sights and sounds that greeted them were worth it all. They alit from the carriage into what seemed to be all of London before them. The members of the *beau monde* were out and about in all their finery, strolling, riding, or driving a curricle down the paths. Within minutes Elizabeth saw a man riding a dandy horse, a lady slapping a gentleman's cheek, and what she thought might have been a prostitute. For the study of the characters about her alone, the day would have been well worth the effort of leaving Gracechurch Street. Against all inclination, Elizabeth found her spirits beginning to rise.

As much as Elizabeth did enjoy herself, she wondered what perverseness within her mind caused her to be always on alert to see *him*. Surely she despised the very notion of laying eyes on him again? Did she not? Yet, over and over, she read his letter. Over and over she heard his words: *"You must allow me to tell you how ardently I admire and love you."*

As they finished an examination of a little shrub by the path, one which Mrs Gardiner thought had very unusual foliage, Elizabeth fancied she could hear his voice, even imagined she could hear him speak her name. She longed to look over her shoulder but did not, telling herself that once she began to heed the directives of voices in her head, then surely she was in real trouble.

"Millie! Millie, not so close to the edge!" Mrs Gardiner sighed. "If she is not just like you, Lizzy, I do not know who is."

Elizabeth chuckled. "We should do best to stand by then, for if she *is* like me, it will take more than Miss Franklin to keep her from falling in."

The two little Gardiner ladies were excited to near raptures by the park. Some young boys their age were sailing boats, and a gentleman was walking about with a poodle on a leash, and they found both crafts and canine enchanting. Mrs Gardiner wore her maternal satisfaction like a mantle, looking down on the sweet picture of her daughters' happiness.

Into this scene, a handsome blond gentleman of unmistakably noble bearing intruded. "I happen to know that dog personally," he informed Elspeth and Millie. "It is perhaps the stupidest creature ever to draw breath. If you would like to meet a dog of *true* worth, I shall retrieve my Florizel from Mayfair to introduce you."

So astonished were the ladies by hearing such an address, and from such an obviously elevated personage, that they stood rooted in silence for a time. It was Jane who first noticed the gentleman who came up behind him.

"Mr Darcy! How do you do, sir?"

Elizabeth barely repressed a gasp as she turned to see him, looking handsomely uncomfortable and staring directly at her. He did not answer Jane. In fact no-one said anything for what seemed an interminable length of time. She would have wagered anything that Mr Darcy would have assiduously avoided her and her sharp tongue. Yet, there he was. Would that she could still be angry at him! But her fury had long since passed, subsumed into the justice of much of his censure and overridden by his declarations of love.

A love which she would have imagined he had put

aside as quickly as he could, save for the fact that he stood before her.

The blond man at last sighed and gave a quick glance heavenward . "Well then, Darcy? You were in such a fever to observe the proprieties, and now you only stand there! Introduce me, man!"

Elizabeth observed in astonishment as Mr Darcy's countenance flushed deep scarlet. He stammered through an awkward presentation of the man whom they soon learnt was his cousin, Viscount Saye, the elder brother of Colonel Fitzwilliam.

"And owner," he informed the two young Miss Gardiners, "of Florizel, a vastly superior beast in both appearance and cleverness to that poodle you so admire." The little ladies giggled.

The viscount was a charming man, as easy and friendly as his brother, and began at once to entertain them all. He proved to be the sort who could make a subject of anything, and soon, they were laughing and talking as if he had known them all since their infancy.

Once he had performed the introductions, Mr Darcy went silent. He stood with his legs unnaturally stiff, one hand gripping his walking stick as his eyes stared blankly at his own feet. After a time, Elizabeth also lapsed into silence, gazing absently over the river and wondering why Mr. Darcy had approached them if, as it seemed, he had no intention of speaking.

It would be his cousin who at last provoked him into

conversation. The viscount was intent on taking them into the rose gardens and would not permit any manner of persuasion against it.

"It is what must be done," announced Lord Saye. "Excessively fashionable. I am sure Mrs Gardiner here would not settle for less. Come, madam, let us take the children. I do not mean to boast but I *am* something of an expert."

This assertion caused Mr Darcy to scoff, albeit quietly, and give a small shake of his head.

With that, Lord Saye took Mrs. Gardiner on his arm, offering his other to Jane. With an unmistakable look of triumph towards his cousin, he set off, motioning Miss Franklin to bring the young Miss Gardiners and come along.

Elizabeth was left alone, standing by the Serpentine with Mr Darcy. She looked at the gentleman whose countenance bore a look of outright humiliation.

He saw her look and lowered his face. "You must forgive my cousin. He has an exuberant character."

"I do not dislike him," Elizabeth replied. Then, in a fit of boldness, she said, "I fear this scheme of his must be more distressing to you than it is to me."

"I am not distressed by it," he said immediately.

"Perhaps, then, we ought to follow them."

To this Mr Darcy offered a small nod and then, hesitantly, extended his arm. She took it, and they began to move, the top of Lord Saye's hat their guide.

CHAPTER THREE

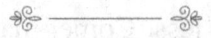

I find myself on Mr Darcy's arm.

It was nothing Elizabeth could ever have imagined when they set out that morning. She could not be easy, not with her own mortification and uncertainty to unsettle her, but neither did she wish him away. She considered, briefly, observing that his exalted cousin seemed quite comfortable with her relations, who were decidedly beneath him, but then thought better of it. Why introduce past injuries when at present there appeared to be some degree of amiability? Alas, it seemed Mr Darcy would introduce it himself.

"How did you say you know Mrs Gardiner?"

She gave him a sidelong glance. "She is my aunt. Her husband is my mother's younger brother."

Mr Darcy did not react visibly, saying only, "She is

very generous to allow us to interrupt your outing as we have."

Elizabeth knew not how to reply and said only very lightly, "Anything to tire the children, or so I have learnt. They live on Gracechurch Street where there are not so many places for children to run and get fresh air."

Mr Darcy said nothing to this.

They seemed to have exhausted the possibility for discourse, and Elizabeth was just about to suggest they pick up their pace to meet the others when Mr Darcy came to a stop.

"Saye thinks..." He faltered, frowned, and jabbed his walking stick at the path.

"Lord Saye thinks...what?"

He drew a deep breath. "My cousin has brought to my attention that it is a particular failing of mine to insist on having the last word in an argument. I had certainly not thought of that consciously, but in retrospect, I can see where it might have seemed that way."

"Where *what* might have seemed *what* way?"

"Giving you a letter and then immediately removing from Kent as I did," he explained. "I was, according to Saye, indulging in my propensity to have the last word."

Elizabeth considered that a moment and began again to move slowly forwards. "It is perhaps a failing but if so, a common one. Do not we all like the final word? We all hope our own opinion or belief is the one that will be proved correct, else we should never undertake to argue for it."

"It is one thing when a person is unable to rebut because your cleverness or reason has rendered them silent; it is quite another when you have silenced them by merely walking away. One can hardly march away victorious when all one has done is refused to allow the potential for response."

"I surely did not feel in any way victorious after that night, sir, and I daresay you did not either." Elizabeth drew a deep breath to quell the emotion which still arose at the thought of their last meeting.

"No, I did not, and I do not still. Nevertheless, we have met again, and I am afforded a second chance to do as I ought to have before and allow you to have your say."

"I have already said too much and been too unjust already. I assure you, sir, I have neither the need nor the wish to say anything more."

"Unjust? Not at all. In fact, I have, in the weeks since we last met, seen a great deal of justice in your feelings. Anything further that you wish to say to me, I am eager to hear." He straightened, as if to gird himself. "You can have nothing to say that I do not deserve, and Saye felt it only right that you be given the opportunity to unburden yourself of whatever bitterness you might harbour towards me."

Elizabeth could only stare, amazed that Mr Darcy, of all people, wished her to deliver him a set-down in the middle of the park. This proud man wanted that she should humiliate him here, surrounded by what seemed to be every person of fashion in London? What did it mean?

"That seems rather impolitic. To what end?"

Mr Darcy seemed to consider that a moment but at length did not directly answer her. Instead, he said only, "Truly, Miss Elizabeth, I urge you to do your worst."

Her laughter seemed to startle him. "Now I know you cannot be in earnest. Not you who knows my worst. You cannot want that, not here, not now."

He nodded, his face set in grim lines. "I do. You would honour me with your candour."

Why? She wanted to press him for an answer. She had departed Kent with no expectation of ever seeing him again. She had imagined he did the same. Why suffer further injury from a person whose acquaintance with you would end? Unless perhaps he did not wish to see their acquaintance ended?

Does he still have hopes where I am concerned?

She had no idea what to think or feel about that—if it were even true.

Nor did she have any notion of what to say to him. His feelings about her family, while not merciful, were certainly just. His rebuke with regard to George

Wickham was well-deserved. As for the matter of Jane and Mr Bingley...

Almost as though he had read her thoughts, he spoke again. "By the bye, I have been unable to see Bingley since my return from Kent, but it is my intention to go to him directly and apprise him of the error I made with regards to your sister. Perhaps I might persuade him to..." His words died. A glance in his direction revealed a furrowed brow and a frown.

"That is to say," he continued, "I have no intention to persuade him to do anything. But if he should hit upon the idea of returning to Hertfordshire...that is to say, I might observe that it would not be a bad idea to return to Hertfordshire...not that I wish to exert undue influence...Bingley, you must understand, is naturally diffident and relies excessively on my judgment, so while I am loath to..."

Very gently, she touched his arm. "I understand. It is good of you to wish to mend that which has been rent, and if it pleases you, I hope you might reassure him that the neighbourhood will be excessively glad to see him return."

He smiled, looking relieved. There was another pause between them. Elizabeth had not the least idea what to say. Had not everything been said? What more could there be?

"Miss Elizabeth," said her companion when the silence had drawn long, "I beg you. Please say whatever you would like to say to me. Say whatever is within your heart. I will bear it cheerfully."

The difficulty with his request was that at present, Elizabeth was unsure *what* was in her heart. In the month since his unexpected declaration to her, she had twisted and turned the events of their prior acquaintance. As she did so, she found her understanding of those events had changed.

I am no longer angry. The understanding did not surprise her, as she was not formed for ill-humour, particularly when the object of her anger appeared before her, seeming penitent. Had he come to her with any measure of his prior arrogance, her former bad feelings might have been bestirred. Instead, he seemed to wish to right prior wrongs, at least insofar as his 'last word' was concerned.

"What have you to say of my insult of you at the assembly in Meryton?" he prompted her. "That was excessively uncivil of me, was it not?"

She turned to see him regarding her with a pointed look. With a grin designed to vex him, she replied airily, "Oh that! So long ago, can it truly signify?"

He did not appear vexed but pursed his lips contemplatively. "I was not very kind to you at Netherfield. I supposed you might have expectations of me if I paid you too much attention."

Elizabeth waved her hand, dismissing that. She was

amused by his dogged attempts to provoke her. "A very reasonable point of view for a man in your position."

"I said such dreadful things about your family."

"And I was rather insolent to yours."

He permitted himself a small smile. "That you were. Fitzwilliam and I had many good laughs for the expression you left on my aunt's face on a number of occasions."

"In any case," she said, swallowing, "you said nothing that was not true. Painful as it was to hear, it was true."

He stopped so suddenly that she was several paces ahead before she halted herself and turned round to see him with a terrible, sorrowful look on his face. For a moment they only beheld one another.

He closed the gap between them, then reached for her hand, pulling it to his lips. "I am sorry. It was not my place, and I beg you would forgive me."

The hand he kissed was at once aglow with a warmth that spread up her arm. Her heart pounded, and she was suddenly quite short of breath. Somehow she managed to utter some syllable or another before again they recovered themselves and walked on.

They had come upon a small knot of parties walking slower than they were, so Elizabeth knew not if it was feeling or necessity that prevented them from speaking for a while. Eventually, they were again relatively alone.

Immediately, Mr Darcy said, "My proposal to you was everything abhorrent."

"Not everything," she said with a smile. "You began well."

"My letter was written in a bitter spirit."

"But the adieu was charity itself."

"This set-down is not going as I believed it would," said Mr Darcy, looking down at her intently. "I should have thought you would be eager to vent your spleen."

"And I would think you might wish to vent yours." She did her best to laugh, but the catch in her throat revealed her true feeling. *Why, why does this man continue to affect me so!* "I am ashamed that I permitted vanity to be my folly. I, who thought myself so wise, such a student of character! I could not see what was before me."

He continued his intent gaze upon her so she added, "Two men, one with merely the appearance of goodness and the other..." Her breath caught again. "The other with the truth of it. You are a good man, Mr Darcy, and I deeply regret I did not before see it."

He seemed as affected as she, though in a different way. He again looked forwards, but save for the movement needed to walk, was utterly still, no movement of breath, or chest, or face to betray his agitation. She wondered, briefly, how he managed such control over his emotions.

At last he said, quietly, "Thank you."

They had, by this time, completely lost sight of Lord

Saye, Jane, her aunt—everyone. Elizabeth made some ridiculous comment wondering where they had got to, and Mr Darcy seemed to understand her discomfiture. He made a remark about quickening their pace, and they did, continuing on in companionable silence.

He shot glances in her direction as they moved through the crowd which she perceived from the corner of her eye. In her mind a resolution was forming, but she knew not if she dared speak it. Would he attend Bingley into Hertfordshire again? Did she want to see him, and if she did, how best to say so? Oh, but the muddle in her mind was dreadful!

After a short time, they met again with the others, and a pleasurable half an hour was spent exclaiming over the sights in the gardens. Too soon, Mrs Gardiner was needed back at home and urged her two nieces to bid their friends farewell. With a surprising amount of regret, Elizabeth did as asked.

Lord Saye made a great scene out of bowing to Elspeth and Millie who giggled and blushed, quite plainly in love with him. To Mrs Gardiner he said, "Madam, I compliment you. I generally find children quite abhorrent, but yours are very charming."

Mr Darcy bowed, looking very serious. Elizabeth had an unanticipated desire to invite him to call on her but did not think it sound to extend the invitation. After all, it was Gracechurch Street. Would he think it beneath his dignity?

In the end, it was Lord Saye who solved her dilemma. "I shall be round with Florizel two days hence, madam, if it should please you."

Mrs Gardiner, to her credit, was neither excessively deferential nor discouraging. She only smiled as though it were her habit to receive viscounts every day. "We shall be honoured to see you."

It had now become far easier for Elizabeth to turn to Darcy and say, "It appears your cousin has an appointment with mine, and if you should find yourself with the inclination to—"

"Georgiana," he said in reply, and she briefly fell silent, so incongruous was the response.

"I beg your pardon, sir?" she finally enquired.

He coloured rather charmingly. "That is to say my sister, Georgiana, would be—you, or rather your aunt— would do me a great honour if you should permit me to bring my sister to meet you."

"You want to bring your sister to Gracechurch Street?"

With almost comical nonchalance that was a direct contrast to his cousin's discomfiture, Lord Saye flung his arm about Darcy's shoulders and answered on his behalf. "Georgiana is going to be almost wild when she finds out we met you today. She has been very nearly frothing at the bit to know you, Miss Elizabeth."

Amused, Elizabeth looked at Mr Darcy to see if he

appeared embarrassed by this assertion, but it did not seem he was.

He gave a small shrug that might have been designed to dislodge his cousin's arm. "If it does not displease you, she has been very eager to know you."

"Then it is settled!" Lord Saye removed his own arm and clapped his hands together. "Until Wednesday, Mrs Gardiner, and allow me to inform you now that I have an unchecked tendency to overstay my welcome."

CHAPTER FOUR

As the gentlemen walked the streets to return to his house, Darcy could not speak for the tumult in his mind. Saye was forbearing for a time—almost until they reached the park gate—but eventually wanted some answers.

"Did you see how fast I walked off with the others?

"Yes."

"Wanted to give you a bit of time with her."

"You are very good, Saye."

"Took her aunt and Miss Bennet right off into the crowd for you. Left you alone with her. Hope you made of it what you could?"

Darcy nodded.

"That Miss Bennet is something to look at, hmm? Silent as a nun though. Then again, I think she has recently had some romantic disappointment."

To this, Darcy could only reply with a disgusted look.

"Ah, right! That was you!" Saye chuckled and gave him a poke on the arm. "Well, not you precisely, but you had a hand in it. Still, I think Bingley ought have ballocks enough to direct his own romances. Why should he be so reliant on your opinion?"

Darcy sighed and tried to walk faster.

"I am sure once Bingley knows how you have bungled your own romance, that will end that! Then again, your problem was that you presumed too much affection, when in his case, you presumed there was none. From what I can see—"

"Saye, enough, I beg you."

That induced a silence that lasted nearly ten paces.

"So, did she give you something of a set-down?"

"A set-down the likes of which Hyde Park has never before seen." Darcy allowed himself a small smile.

"Ah!" Saye nodded, his eyes bright with anticipation. Clearly, he expected more information to be forthcoming.

They had then arrived at Darcy's door. They entered, handing off coats, hats, and gloves to Darcy's housekeeper who asked if they would like something to eat. Saye immediately replied that he would, very passionately, appreciate some tea and fruit, and if some meat and cheese happened upon the plate, so much the better.

Darcy began moving down the hall towards the

drawing room, Saye keeping pace beside him. "What did she say?"

"Mrs Hobbs? She said she would bring the food to the drawing room."

"Not Hobbs. Miss Elizabeth Bennet! Did she take you to task? Or had she more to say of your dreadful offer?"

Darcy shrugged. "Oh, she said a little of this and a little of that."

Behind him, Saye cursed. They had arrived in the drawing room by then where, as he had hoped, Georgiana sat with a book. He greeted her with a kiss on her cheek and sat down near her, informing her of the repast that was on its way to them. All the time, Saye stood indignantly in the centre of the room, nearly twitching with fury.

"Devil take it, Darcy!" he bellowed at last.

"Mind your tongue," Darcy admonished. "We are in the presence of a lady."

"Think nothing of it," Georgiana assured him, looking baffled but interested by the goings-on.

"This is all quite ungenerous of you! It was I who formed the design of this whole plot. I have been hearing your moaning and wailing for weeks about this girl, and then, just when I have arranged everything for you, you go silent! Have you no feeling for the needs of others?"

"Feeling for the needs of others?" Darcy asked. "You *need* to know my most private affairs?"

"Yes, I do," Saye retorted. He came forwards quickly and grabbed Georgiana's book. "Imagine if I should hurl this directly into the fire? You would never know how it ended!"

"In truth, I have read it before," Georgiana replied sweetly. "But I should think it a dreadful waste nevertheless."

"I feel," Saye enunciated carefully, tapping the book with each word, "as though I were reading a book and someone came and tossed it into the fire before I knew the ending. Is that just? Where is your sense of what is honourable and good?"

"Miss Elizabeth Bennet and I are hardly arrived at our last chapter," he said. "At least I hope we have not."

There was another brief silence in which Saye tossed himself into a chair, huffing and puffing angrily, giving Darcy many sidelong scowls and muttering about ingratitude and the respect due an elder cousin.

"Miss Elizabeth Bennet? Have you met her again?" Georgiana enquired.

Georgiana did not know the specifics of his time in Kent, or at least he had not spoken of it to her. It would not be beyond Fitzwilliam or Saye to apprise her of all the news he did not wish his young sister to hear. But she was not blind and had likely observed his melan-

choly, inasmuch as even now, she might have perceived
the sudden removal of it.

"I have, and she has invited us to call on her in
Gracechurch Street two days hence. The bellows on the
chair over there will come along to show off his dog
while you and I visit with Miss Elizabeth. Does that suit
you?"

Georgiana turned pink and pressed her lips together
before allowing a beaming smile to break across her
countenance. She then replied with effusions of pleasure, leaving him quite certain of how very much the
plan *did* suit her. Moments later, refusing any part of the
repast that Mrs Hobbs brought in for the gentlemen, she
nearly skipped from the room, intent on examining her
gowns so that she might determine what to wear to
Gracechurch Street.

"Just tell me part of what she said," Saye wheedled as
soon as she was gone.

"Very well. She said the neighbourhood would be
glad to see Bingley return." Recollecting that made some
of Darcy's hope dissipate.

"Very good, yes?"

Darcy shook his head. "Not good at all, in fact. I
wonder if he might have met someone in Scarborough. I
had one of his letters from him waiting when I returned
from Kent. It was difficult to discern the particulars, but
it seemed he was attending a great many parties."

Saye seemed to understand the problem at once.

"Much opportunity for new love in two months, particularly for the callow sort."

"As agreeable as she was in the park," Darcy observed glumly, "further disappointment for her sister will likely put an end to it. I should guarantee it, in fact."

"How are you so certain?"

"She said so. That night at Hunsford she said, 'Had not my own feelings decided against you…had they even been favourable, do you think that any consideration would tempt me to accept the man, who has been the means of ruining, perhaps forever, the happiness of a most beloved sister?' This matter of her sister's happiness must be completed before she would even consider another proposal from me."

Saye appeared to think it less a problem than Darcy, if his yawn was any indication. "So summon Bingley. Let us get him in hand, and we will take him with us to Gracechurch Street."

"And if his affections have wavered?"

Saye shrugged. "A problem for tomorrow."

Mrs Gardiner and Jane both forbore to ask questions until they were all delivered into Mrs Gardiner's parlour. Just enough time elapsed that Elizabeth had begun to hope she would not be called upon for explanations—when suddenly, she was.

"Well, Lizzy," said Mrs Gardiner whilst pouring tea, "our time at the park was certainly unusual."

Elizabeth accepted a cup from her aunt and raised it to her lips, wishing to have time to form her reply.

"Lord Saye was very agreeable and absolutely charming with the children," she added. "I suppose it must have been due to my beauty that he spent so much time with us."

Both of her nieces giggled at that, and Elizabeth felt colour come to her cheeks but still could say nothing of sense about the real subject.

"Perhaps it was," she replied lightly, "after all, you are scarcely thirty and look five years less. My uncle is a fortunate man."

"Lizzy," Jane said, more easily exasperated than their aunt. "We were not five minutes with his lordship when we understood that his true object was to leave Mr Darcy alone with you. Now why should that be?"

"I am not sure myself."

Frustration appeared on both of her companions' countenances, in the form of pressed-together lips on Mrs Gardiner and a sigh from Jane. Thus, with halting candour, Elizabeth told them all, from meeting him in the parsonage, walking with him in the grounds of Rosings Park, his shocking proposal, and her vitriolic reply. "After all that, I am utterly amazed he does not despise me."

"As am I. It speaks well of his character that he does

not. It seems to me as though he would like to show you he is different than you thought," Mrs Gardiner replied.

"I do not know about that. His cousin tasked him with being excessively prone towards having the last word in an argument, so he wished to offer me the opportunity to reply to his letter. Perhaps he wanted nothing more than to prove his cousin incorrect or even to prove me incorrect."

"He does not need to bring his sister to Gracechurch Street to prove anything to his cousin, or to you," Jane observed.

"True, but I am disinclined to make too much of it."

"There is no conclusion here but to see he is still in love with you," Jane insisted.

Elizabeth's instinct was to demur but found she could not, mostly because she could not think of another reason for Mr Darcy's actions and behaviour.

"The question for you, Lizzy, is how do you feel about it all?" Mrs Gardiner asked.

Elizabeth opened her mouth, then reconsidered and closed it again. Then she said, "If you had asked me that question a month ago I would have told you that Mr Darcy was a hateful man and the last man in the world I could ever marry."

"I am not asking the question a month ago," Mrs Gardiner said. "I am asking it now."

"While we walked, Lord Saye confided that Mr Darcy

has been engaged in a course of self-improvement. We knew not the reasons behind it, of course."

"Oh!" Elizabeth blushed hotly. "Well...the conduct of neither of us, if strictly examined, will prove irreproachable. The fact is that I believe I have grossly misjudged him, and it is pleasing to hope I may have a chance to begin anew."

"He truly has no improper pride," Jane mused, her voice sounding contemplative. "No man who did could go to a woman who had scorned him so violently as you."

Elizabeth took a drink of her tea and swallowed audibly. "No, I see that now. For whatever ill feelings that night engendered in him, they were quickly set aside by his...well, by, um, I guess you would say—"

"Love," Jane said again, more forcefully this time. "Ardent love. Unshakeable, ardent love."

Feeling decidedly ill at ease, Elizabeth said only, "Maybe."

"I believe she is correct," Mrs Gardiner said. "And so we can only come back to you, Elizabeth. What is it that you want in all of this?"

Elizabeth set her teacup down in its saucer. Considering it for a moment, she said, "I truly cannot say."

CHAPTER FIVE

"We can take two carriages," Saye announced firmly the next morning.

A group had convened at Darcy's breakfast table, each of them seeming to have some reason or another that they needed to call on Miss Elizabeth Bennet on Gracechurch Street.

When I imagined the difficulties my relations might have with Elizabeth's relations, Darcy thought grimly, *all of them wishing to call on them at once was not one of them.*

"I refuse to descend on Gracechurch Street like a herd of cattle," Darcy said firmly. "It is unseemly to go to a place like that with a multitude of carriages, as though we think ourselves royalty on an alms visit."

"Neither can we shove six of us in one carriage," Saye replied. "You are the one who insists on bringing

Bingley, and Florizel dislikes being crammed and jammed."

"By all means we should defer to Florizel's needs," Colonel Fitzwilliam interjected, helping himself to more ham.

"Not everyone needs to go," Darcy insisted. "It is not a party. Just a simple morning call!"

"Bingley is the problem," Saye told him. "He always lolls in a carriage—takes up an extraordinary amount of space for such a slender person."

"Bingley has purpose there," Darcy replied. "I am sorry but if the only purpose in going is to meet Miss Elizabeth again—"

"So everyone is invited but me? That hardly seems fair," Fitzwilliam said, placing his fork down with a piqued clatter. "I daresay I know her better than most anyone here, and unlike some, I have never insulted her relations."

"Your pout is a shocking contrast to your regimentals," his brother informed him. "Like a silver saddle on a donkey."

Georgiana had been quietly attending to her toast throughout. "I do not wish to be left behind, but if needed, I can go to her another day?" The disappointment in her eyes clearly spoke to how much such an offer had cost her.

"No. You are most certainly one of the party. She is eager to meet you," Darcy reassured her.

"They leave on Friday to return to Hertfordshire," Saye informed them, causing Darcy's heart to drop. He had not known it himself, and it placed an even greater importance on the call.

"Either we call tomorrow," Saye continued, "or the opportunity is lost."

"Very well, we all go, all pressed into one carriage like the mail stage from Birmingham," Darcy said.

Mr Darcy is not best pleased to be here.

The group from Grosvenor Square, larger than either Elizabeth or her aunt had expected, arrived just before the noon hour. The call had not begun auspiciously.

Mr Bingley, it seemed, had been unable to join them, plunging Jane into an immediate and thorough melancholic silence. Lord Saye's dog, Florizel, had entered the Gardiners' home and immediately soiled the drawing room carpet. Little Millie, enchanted and heedless, had dropped to her knees to hug him, landing squarely on the foul little pile. Lord Saye was mortified and apologetic and wished to send for his purse, wanting to replace the entire carpet, which Mrs Gardiner assured him was not at all necessary. Miss Darcy appeared to be in agony at the whole of it. Her face had flamed red, and she could barely stutter out a greeting to any of them. Mr Darcy had gone pale with rage and then stalked to the window, putting his back to the room.

Elizabeth had been pleased by Mr and Mrs Gardiner, who showed their innate good manners, quietly summoning the housekeeper and a maid to take care of the carpet and Millie, while Mr Gardiner's man, Huxley, took Florizel outside to be certain nothing further was forthcoming. Elspeth accompanied Huxley and her sister, and the room was restored to some semblance of serenity.

Mr Gardiner went at once to Mr Darcy and the other two gentleman, and in short time, they had all had retired to her uncle's book room on the pretence of looking at some book or the like. Elizabeth found herself drawn to Miss Darcy, who had remained in unspeaking mortification in her chair.

"I am so delighted you came this morning," she said. "I have long wished to meet you."

"You have?" The girl seemed unduly startled by this assertion. "I have wished to meet you as well."

"Then we must get to know one another." Elizabeth angled her body such that Jane might be included in the conversation, but Jane only smiled faintly and dropped her gaze without uttering a syllable. Repressing a sigh of frustration, Elizabeth returned her attentions to Miss Darcy.

Though it began haltingly, Elizabeth found she was soon able to draw the girl out a bit by canvassing the most banal of subjects—music and books, how she liked her home in Pemberley compared to town, and what she liked best to do when she was there.

Strangely, the answer seemed to be not much at all. Miss Darcy, Elizabeth concluded, was painfully shy, and her reserve had not been helped at her school, where most of the young ladies thought her haughty and did not befriend her.

But Elizabeth found that she liked her very well. What might have been perceived as hauteur was merely reticence misunderstood, and with a jolt, she wondered how that might be applied to her brother as well. With enough time and the gentle application of her own talent of conversing, she and Miss Darcy were soon chatting like old friends.

When the gentlemen joined them again, Elizabeth found herself strangely disappointed that Mr Darcy did not sit with her. He seemed to have found a true kinship with Mr Gardiner, and the two of them sat in a corner speaking animatedly about angling while Mrs Gardiner served refreshments and tea.

Why did he come? All of the prior conclusions of her aunt and Jane—that he must somehow still love her—seemed now patently false. He had scarcely spoken to her and rarely even looked at her. She did notice that, more than once, he glanced at Jane, seeming to take the measure of her. Had he come on some sort of reconnaissance mission for his friend, trying to gauge whether Elizabeth's assertions of Jane's heartbreak were true?

"I understand, Miss Elizabeth, that you and your sister are to return to Hertfordshire soon?"

Elizabeth jumped a little guiltily, hoping she had not neglected her new friend too grievously. "The day after tomorrow. My father is to arrive later tonight but wishes to spend a day with his brother-in-law tomorrow. So we will depart on Friday."

"I wish you safe travel." Miss Darcy glanced towards the rest of her party. The gentlemen had risen. Reluctantly, Florizel had been handed into the care of his master. Elspeth and Millie had been with him in the kitchens, playing, petting, and no doubt feeding him treat after treat. The poor animal was nearly falling asleep where he stood.

As they bid their guests farewell, Mr Darcy bowed to Elizabeth with no particular warmth in his demeanour. When she heard the sound of the front door closing behind them, she went to the window to see them leave, something like regret causing an ache in her heart.

Of them all, Darcy was the only one in low spirits as the carriage began its journey back to Mayfair. Never before had he felt more foolish, more humiliated for his own pretensions. Even if he and Elizabeth had spoken lightly of it in the park, he burned with the shame of it now. As God was his witness, he would have gladly been related to the Gardiners rather than Lady Catherine and the circus which accompanied him even now. He sent his most baleful glare towards Florizel who was snoring happily on the bench across from him.

"Well, that Gardiner was a fine fellow, did you not think?" Fitzwilliam grinned happily around the carriage. "Very gentleman-like. I did not expect him to be so young."

"He will be thirty-five on his next birthday," Saye informed them all. "Mrs Gardiner is younger than you are, Richard."

"And quite pretty," Fitzwilliam concluded. "She is from Lambton, Darcy. Did you know that? I should not be surprised if you had seen her at church or something while she was young."

"I might buy a place down there," Saye announced.

"Down where?" Darcy asked.

"Gracechurch Street. The very place we just left! I could do as Gardiner did, get three houses for a song and knock the walls down in between."

"Why would you buy a place there? Charming, but hardly fashionable," Fitzwilliam said.

"Because people who follow fashion are sheep, and I am the shepherd." Saye grinned. "And I would like to see if they will follow me to Gracechurch Street. Sir Frederick would be there within the week. I would wager all I have on it. Besides, what about my sons?"

"What about your *wife?*" His brother retorted. "Need one of those before you are worrying about any sons."

"I am going to have a number of sons," Saye replied with blithe confidence. "Three, probably four, and they will need places to live. I need to buy in before these hordes of noblemen come in and drive the prices up."

"What makes you think you will have so many sons?" Fitzwilliam asked.

"'Tis all a ratio," Saye informed him. He gestured towards the fall of his breeches in a manner he no doubt thought was discreet. "You compare the measurement of prince to pudding, and that is how one knows how many sons one will father."

"Pray recollect there is a young lady with us," Darcy interrupted tiredly.

"She is fourteen now and—" Saye began.

"Fourteen!" Georgiana interrupted indignantly. "I should say not. I am sixteen."

"Sixteen!" Saye gave her a mockingly incredulous look. "Impossible. In fact, I thought you to were thirteen but said fourteen to flatter you."

Darcy hoped such teasing would not upset his sister, but Georgiana surprised him. With a sweet smile, she said, "No doubt it is a sign of your advancing age that your vision fails you so."

"The impertinence! No supper for you, miss," Saye roared good-naturedly.

It was a delight to them all. Teasing was never something Georgiana managed easily. Most of it directed at her left her in tears. To see her not only bearing it but returning her own was nothing short of marvellous.

No doubt a teasing elder sister would be of great use in that quarter. That thought returned Darcy immediately to his despondency.

"Did you enjoy yourself, Georgiana?" he asked quietly.

"I did, very much." Her eyes shone as she turned to him. "I think she liked me."

"Miss Elizabeth Bennet?"

She nodded eagerly.

"Why, of course she did. I could see it plain. But did you like her?"

"Oh very much so. I hope..." Georgiana peered more closely at him. "I hope I might meet her again. She means to travel to the Lakes with her aunt and uncle later in the summer, and I thought perhaps they could be persuaded to stop at Pemberley and see us."

"I think we can depend upon it," Darcy assured her. Mr Gardiner said they meant to go in July. Darcy had not thought twice before extending an invitation to him to fish in his trout stream, and Mr Gardiner had accepted with delight.

Alas, that pleasure was to be had two long months

hence, months during which any number of suitors might introduce themselves to his Elizabeth and steal her away, as had happened in Bingley's case.

He frowned, recollecting his conversation the day prior with Bingley. He had gone to his friend's rooms fully prepared to confess his wrongdoing where Miss Bennet was concerned. Bingley had met him with a beaming smile and tales of a new lady-love that he had met while visiting his family in Scarborough. Miss Edwina Thorne was a wealthy young woman whose father had lately been knighted. She was age eighteen and "an absolute angel, Darcy. A lady beyond compare."

It seemed that Bingley had decided he must put his attraction for Miss Jane Bennet behind him and had gone north hoping to meet another. *And so he had*, Darcy thought grimly.

Darcy had gone ahead with his confession to Bingley as planned. He had included with it the report that he had met the Miss Bennets lately in London, and it appeared that Miss Jane Bennet was low in spirits. With great diffidence he had said, "I do not mean to interfere again, but it does seem the lady may be yet affected by her feelings where you are concerned."

Bingley had considered this for a time before concluding, "Be that as it may, Darcy, I have given this matter a great deal of thought. Even if you were mistaken, would not others think the same?"

Darcy had tried to protest. "We were all mistaken—"

"But if you, who were there—you, who attended the parties, saw us together for above two months—if *you* could not see the attachment, then would anyone? I should despise being out and about in London with everyone thinking my wife did not truly love me or only loved my wealth."

And so that was that. Bingley had neither immediate plans nor the inclination to return to Hertfordshire, and thus, neither did Darcy.

Pemberley is the only hope, he mused, his eyes resting on his sister. *Georgiana must prevail upon Elizabeth to come to Pemberley with her aunt and uncle.*

CHAPTER SIX

"What say you to this morning?" Mr Gardiner asked jovially when the guests had gone. He had enjoyed a fine hour. The promise of fishing Pemberley's streams, however distant, was enough to ensure his satisfaction. "Save for the carpet, I should call it a success."

"Lord Saye is certainly eccentric, and the carpet cleaned up perfectly well," Mrs Gardiner replied.

"These young noblemen will behave as they please," her husband assured her, "but he was amiable and had the grace to be embarrassed by his pet. I saw nothing to dislike in his manners."

Both Gardiners then rose, intending to go about their respective day's occupations, while Jane and Elizabeth remained behind, enjoying the sunshine in their aunt's drawing room.

"What did you think, Lizzy?" Jane asked softly. It was the first sentence she had uttered since the group had arrived without Mr Bingley.

Elizabeth could only shake her head, her disappointment acute. Mr Darcy had been reticent and aloof, and Mr Bingley had not come. In short, she did not see that either she or her sister had anything to hope for with either gentleman.

"I hardly know what to say," she finally answered. "Mr Darcy was surely no lover today."

"I still say his affections and wishes for you are unchanged. This call, introducing you to his sister, makes no sense otherwise."

"Perhaps he wished only for a friend for Miss Darcy? She mentioned that she has few enough of those," Elizabeth suggested lightly.

Jane rolled her eyes at that. "What good would having a friend in Hertfordshire do her?"

"You saw how he was. I doubt Mr Darcy said three words to me."

Jane could not dispute that and so only returned a wry smile. "Maybe you will see him at Pemberley, then? It seems our uncle means to go."

Elizabeth did long to go to Pemberley. Who would not wish to see the place of which she had heard so much? But did she wish to see *him* again? It was all such bafflement, to swing so madly from hatred of a man to... whatever it was she felt now. The only thing Elizabeth could say with certainty was that without more time to spend in his company, she would likely never know what might have been.

Mr Bennet arrived at the expected hour, which was near to dinner time. He was out of sorts at first, as was commonplace when he was required to come to London, but cheered quickly once he saw the new books Mr Gardiner had procured on his behalf.

"A full stomach, a glass of your port, and these," he said, raising said glass to his host. "You have done me well, sir, and taken excellent care of my girls too."

All of that said, Elizabeth did not deceive herself. Mr Bennet had sent more than one quizzical glance in her direction during dinner when her laugh had been too late or too forced, or when he expected her interest and got none. She was not nearly so dreary as Jane, but she lacked her customary vivacity and was, therefore, unsurprised when Mr Bennet took her aside after dinner.

"Dear Lizzy," said Mr Bennet when they were alone, closeted in Mr Gardiner's book room. "I must admit to some fatherly concern on seeing you. It does not appear that a month in town has done you much good. Or was it the time spent in Mr Collins's home that has you so altered?"

"A-am I altered?" Elizabeth raised her hand to her

hair, tugging at the curl on the nape of her neck. "Perhaps I just look a little pale. It has rained a great deal of late."

Mr Bennet gave her a considering look. "You do not appear to have been sleeping or eating well. Am I incorrect?"

After a short debate within herself, she decided she would confide in him. Mrs Gardiner and Jane were likely to paint a pretty picture of the matter, but in her father, she knew she could depend upon honesty, even if he spoke a truth she did not wish to hear.

Elizabeth sighed. "I must confess it is neither town nor Mr Collins to blame for my present state. I fear you will be deeply shocked when you hear what is responsible."

She told him everything then, sparing no detail: what Mr Darcy had said, what she had said, her feelings after that, and then, how it was upon seeing him again both in the park and when he and his relations called in Gracechurch Street.

Upon hearing of the illustrious personages that had been there only hours prior, Mr Bennet gave a little snort of disbelief. "Mr Darcy on Gracechurch Street! Now, there is a sight I should have liked to witness. No doubt he has been cleansing himself of the experience ever since."

Elizabeth frowned. It was a more bitter rejoinder than she might have anticipated. "In fact he was very amiable—my uncle was exceedingly pleased with him. His family were all very good, too, if somewhat..." She considered for a moment before concluding, "Eccentric."

Her father removed his spectacles, using his neck-cloth to rub the glass a moment before replacing them on his nose. "Hmm. Well, it seems I missed the opportunity to study some very peculiar characters. In any case, I still fail to comprehend why any of this should cause you to lose sleep or put you off your meals."

"Because I...I fear I made a mistake. Nay, I *did* make a mistake."

Mr Bennet's attention, which had begun to drift towards the reading materials laid out on the side table, snapped back towards her. "Mistake? What do you mean?"

Elizabeth realised that she was jiggling her left foot madly, and it was making her entire body shake. She forced herself to stop. "I...I wonder if my feelings for the gentleman might be somewhat...not...that is, unlike... he was just so altered! And I realised I had misunderstood—"

"Hear me now, Elizabeth," Mr Bennet said, and she recoiled from the sternness in his tone. "Do not have your head turned simply because Mr Darcy has arrived on Gracechurch Street in a fine carriage with his fashionable cousins."

"Mr Darcy was in the very same carriage he had brought to Hertfordshire and to Kent," she protested, a dull heat rising up her chest at her father's censuring tone.

"I know how it is, my girl. Lady Catherine was a grand personage, and then you were in Hyde Park, seeing all the highest of the high parading their wealth about. It was natural you should begin to think such a life might be quite agreeable."

"Pray credit me with more wit than that. You surely do not think it is Mr Darcy's riches that have altered my opinion of him? Because I can assure you, I knew Mr Darcy was wealthy the very night I met him and—"

"The night he insulted you?"

"He wounded my vanity, and I have assiduously punished him for that infraction since!" Elizabeth took a deep breath that did nothing to calm her rising agitation. "The mistake I made was in allowing that one event to forever alter my opinion of him. I became prejudiced against a man who is—"

"Disagreeable on his best days," Mr Bennet concluded.

"No! No, that is not—he is far different than ever I knew. He is a very good man. And what has kept me awake at night is wondering exactly what my feelings are or might have been for him, what chance at happiness I might have missed but for my own stubborn pride."

Mr Bennet closed his eyes and leant back his head back for several seconds. When he opened them again, he spoke in a tone that was more peaceable, even if the words he uttered were not.

"We need not argue for the past, child. It cannot signify. He is gone now, and it is highly unlikely you will meet him again."

"I hope that is not true." The words came out before she could stop them.

"Maybe next Easter, if you go to the Collinses again—"

"He has invited Uncle Gardiner to come fish with him at Pemberley when we travel this summer."

Her father's face hardened. "I fail to see what your uncle's fishing plans should have to do with you."

"No doubt Mrs Gardiner and I shall call on Miss Darcy, who is a delightful girl," Elizabeth explained. "And if I should meet her brother then I shall be well prepared for...whatever may happen."

Her father's jaw dropped, and he stared at her for a moment. "You surely cannot mean that you would give that proud, unpleasant man a second chance? Yes, marriage to a man like that would bring with it elegant carriages and luxurious homes, but do not make me think so little of you to imagine those things would make you accept such a man."

"Papa, I just said his wealth has positively nothing to do with it! What I mean to say is that were things this summer to occur such that we, having each a better understanding of the other, came to any sort of—"

Her father held up one hand. "I shall stop you right there. I am not sending you off all summer so that you may have your head turned by Mr Darcy's estate. See what even this sojourn into Kent has done to your mind!"

"Should I find Pemberley to be a ramshackle peasant cottage, it will not change my opinion in the least," she said, wishing to raise her voice but determined to speak in an even tone. "I have learnt that Mr Darcy is, in fact, not proud, not disagreeable, and not at all unpleasant. Indeed, he is perfectly amiable and has no improper pride, and should he be so inclined as to offer for me—"

"Elizabeth, you have absolutely lost your mind," her father said sternly.

"In fact, I have a better understanding of my mind than ever before. Do you not see how I was to him? Are you not ashamed of me? I was blind, partial, prejudiced and absurd! Taken in by Mr Wickham because he flattered me, while taking a fervent dislike to Mr Darcy simply because he insulted my beauty!"

"It does not signify. You could never be happy with a man like Mr Darcy. You will never be happy unless you truly esteem your husband and can look up to him as your superior. Your lively talents would place you in the greatest danger in an unequal marriage."

"I cannot say I wholly comprehend the implication in such a statement," Elizabeth said stiffly, "but I assure you, nothing but esteem would persuade me to marry any man, much less Mr Darcy."

"Whom we both know you hate."

Now she did raise her voice for it seemed her father was determined to wilfully mishear her. "No, I do *not*. Not even a little. In fact, I think Mr Darcy just might be the man who in disposition, talent, and understanding of the world, suits me better than any other ever could."

"This is absolute nonsense. I am ashamed of you, Lizzy. You are being unnecessarily obstinate." Mr Bennet shook a finger at her while he spoke. "While I still draw breath, you will not marry Mr Darcy or even entertain further discourse with him."

To this, Elizabeth only dropped her eyes and shrugged, maintaining an indifferent posture throughout the pause which ensued. She looked up again when her father resumed speaking.

"You must promise me that you will never, ever consider another proposal from Mr Darcy," said Mr Bennet, danger making his eyes dark, "or you will not be permitted to go with the Gardiners this summer. Or, for that matter, visit them in town."

Her emotions threatened to overflow into tears, and that she could not abide. She was not sad; she was enraged. Yet, what could be done?

If I do not make this promise to Papa, he will keep me home, in which case, he gets his way, for I shall likely never see Mr

Darcy again. And if I do give my word, then...well, then I might meet him again but if he was predisposed to renew his offer...

She could not think of that. If Mr Darcy proposed again, she would consider it. Nay, she would...consent to it?

"I cannot, in good conscience, make a promise to you that I know, even now, is a lie."

"Elizabeth, think of what you say!"

"I am thinking of what I say," she replied evenly, rising from her chair. "I will go to my aunt now and tell her that regretfully, I am unable to accompany them to the Lakes this summer."

"Tell them to take Jane," Mr Bennet said, his usual satire sounding cruel. "No doubt they would prefer to take the sensible daughter."

CHAPTER SEVEN

"It was something of a spectacle, I shall grant you that," Fitzwilliam admitted as he and Darcy walked towards their club the day after their visit to Gracechurch Street. "Still, I do not see why you had to go silent as you did."

"Can you not?" Darcy shook his head. "Firstly, I arrived already knowing I must disappoint further her beloved sister, for Bingley has done as Bingley tends to do and transferred his affections to another lady. But then, as though that were not bad enough, having been so harsh about her family—I brought Bedlam with me!"

Fitzwilliam could merely offer a sympathetic wince to that.

"And it is *her* relations, the very genteel and charming Gardiners—upon whom I have heaped endless scorn—

who are required to overlook our offences. There could not have been a more poignant example of my idiocy!"

"Be an idiot then." Fitzwilliam shrugged. "The way I see it, either you take a chance now—"

"No, no, no," Darcy interrupted him. "I have thought on it, and truly, my only hope is this travel to Derbyshire that is planned for the summer. Two months hence! I despise the very idea of it, but it is my best hope."

They had arrived at the club and entered, handing coats, hats, and walking sticks to the waiting servant.

"His lordship said to meet him at his usual table," Fitzwilliam said.

Unlike most noblemen, Lord Matlock thought it foppish to jostle for position in the window of his club. He preferred the dark recesses at the back. The pair moved through the long room, passing by table after table, nodding to acquaintances.

When they were about halfway through, Darcy was arrested by a pair of fine eyes in the face of an...older gentleman?

I had not before noticed that father and daughter shared the same eyes, he thought.

"Go on, I will join you in a bit," he murmured to his cousin, then approached Mr Bennet's table.

"How do you do, good sir?" he said awkwardly.

"Mr Darcy." Mr Bennet nodded. He was seated beside Sir Archibald Lawson. Darcy knew the man also and greeted him, after which Sir Archibald rose and gestured to Darcy to take his seat.

"Entertain Bennet for me," he said. "I need to speak to Lord Elton."

Mr Bennet frowned slightly, seeming to dislike the idea, but regardless, Darcy sat. If he were ever to win Elizabeth's hand, he reasoned, having her father's good opinion would be paramount. As the gentleman made idle conversation, however, Darcy began to wonder if that would be possible. Mr Bennet was, at best, ill at ease; at worst, outright hostile. Had he been such a beast in Hertfordshire to warrant the gentleman's ire?

Yes, yes you were. You insulted this man's favoured daughter, and no doubt he has heard much of every ill opinion she ever held of you.

Darcy knew not how to rectify that. Their conversation had languished and Mr Bennet, it seemed, was perfectly content to pretend Darcy was not even there. He had turned his head away, his eyes wandering aimlessly over the rest of the room. With this, Darcy formed a resolution. Candour was in every way against his nature, but candour was required.

"Sir?" When Mr Bennet looked at him, Darcy continued. "It has um, occurred to me of late that I was somewhat ill mannered towards you and your family last autumn."

"Occurred to you?" Mr Bennet chuckled. "Do you mean when Elizabeth *told* you?"

Had she confided in her father about his proposal? Darcy swallowed, glancing quickly about the room. Thankfully, it was less occupied than usual. "Yes. I daresay your daughter has told you of the...um, about our meeting in Kent?"

"One meeting in particular in my cousin's home."

"It was badly done," Darcy said. "I assure you I am mortified by my conduct towards her. Miss Elizabeth taught me a lesson, hard indeed at first, but most advantageous. By her, I have been properly humbled."

"Well," said Mr Bennet, seeming not to know what to say to that. "I have heard much from my daughter on the manner in which she has misunderstood you, so it seems you have both been, in turns, led to understand each other and yourselves better."

Encouraged, Darcy nodded. "I cannot disagree. And it is my hope that on further acquaintance, we might—"

"There will not be any further acquaintance," Mr Bennet replied shortly. "I understand that Mr Bingley has given up Netherfield Park."

"You know more than I do, then."

"I have heard that a family called Bickford will be there by the next quarter day. So you see, Mr Darcy, the intersection of our families has come to its natural end. We will, as ever, wish you well." He smiled blandly, looking the very opposite of a person who wished another well.

"Save for this summer," Darcy replied, studying Mr

Bennet as he did. He had never before said such things to any father, never wanting to give another man the least hope where a daughter was concerned. Ironic that the very man he hoped to one day call his father-in-law seemed determined to ignore his implications.

"Hmm?"

"This summer when Miss Elizabeth travels to Derbyshire with Mr and Mrs Gardiner." With a determined smile he added, "It is my dearest wish that they will spend time with us at Pemberley."

"Elizabeth will not be travelling with her aunt and uncle this summer."

"I had understood—"

"I have decided that it is inadvisable that she should go," Mr Bennet said impatiently.

"How so?" Darcy pressed. He suspected he was being somewhat impudent but found he did not much care.

"It just is."

The two men sat eyeing one another until Darcy said, "Travel is an excellent thing for a lady, particularly one with a spirit and a curiosity such as your daughter. I cannot think she much likes the idea of missing the opportunity."

"She gave it up readily enough."

"That does surprise me."

"Elizabeth can be very stubborn. She will do much to carry her point."

Darcy sat back, his mind racing to keep up with what

he instinctively knew was important to him. "And what was the point she wished to carry?"

Mr Bennet waved his hand. "It does not signify. A bit of nonsense."

"It must have been an important point indeed if she gave up the opportunity to travel with beloved relations to carry it."

"As you may be aware," Mr Bennet said, enunciating clearly, "when Elizabeth's character is called into question, she reacts rather violently, even if it means defending an opinion that is not necessarily true."

"It seems peculiar to me that you of all people should question her character."

Mr Bennet pointed a finger at him. "I will not have my daughter's head turned by a pack of dandies in Hyde Park or fine carriages and an earl's sons calling at Gracechurch Street."

Darcy considered that a moment. Was Mr Bennet implying that Elizabeth had changed her opinion of him because of the events in London?

"You judge her ill if you suppose that any of those sorts of things would alter any opinion she has of me," he said at last. "Miss Elizabeth has known my exact income since the very first moment of our acquaintance, and it has persuaded her not a jot for many months."

A servant came to the table near them, clearing away plates and cups left by the previous gentleman. Mr Bennet watched him as if it were the most fascinating sight in the world. Darcy was perfectly content to wait out the silence.

At last he sighed heavily. "Mr Darcy, I do not mean to insult you or my daughter, whom I love dearly. What I will say is that an alteration in opinion is one thing, but marriage is quite another. Elizabeth looked positively ill when I saw her. She has clearly not slept well, nor does it appear her appetite has been good. This...this business between you has troubled her and left her out of sorts, and therefore, I believe it is not good for her."

Yes, it has troubled me too, Darcy thought even as his heart leapt at the idea that Elizabeth was, in any small part, feeling regret. His own waistcoats were feeling looser these days, and as for sleep, four or five hours had become a good night's rest for him.

"All that I asked of her was that she put this nonsense behind her. I said that in order to be allowed to go with her aunt and uncle this summer, she needed to promise me no such silliness would arise again. Specifically, I said that yes, she could go with the Gardiners, but only if she would promise me that any notion of engagement or marriage to you be forsworn."

Darcy felt his heart begin to pound violently. "Do you mean to say that the condition you imposed upon her was that she be absolutely, positively sworn against me?"

Mr Bennet peered at him closely from over his spectacles. "Understand that I mean no injury to you, sir. My daughter's head has been turned—by what I cannot say —but it does her ill. Until I can be certain she will be sensible about the world, and her place within it, I must keep her at home."

The idea of Mr Bennet thinking that Elizabeth was behaving nonsensically was utter rot, but Darcy could not think of it. There was a matter far more interesting to him at hand.

"To be clear, sir, you wanted her to promise that she would absolutely put out of her mind any notion of an engagement with me—*ever*—else she could not go on holiday with her aunt and uncle? The only way she would be permitted to go was if she promised you that, yes? And what did she say to that?"

Mr Bennet paused, drumming his fingers on the table briefly before admitting, "She said no. She would not promise me that she would not entertain a second offer of marriage from you and said she would rather remain at home than make a vow she had no intention of upholding."

Darcy arose with such rapidity that his chair nearly toppled. He waved to the servant, demanding his coat and hat be brought at once. "Meet me by the entrance," he told the boy. "Make haste."

"Mr Darcy, where do you go?" asked Mr Bennet, half-rising out of his own chair.

With a broad smile, Darcy informed him, "Gracechurch Street."

"That would certainly be a waste of your time."

At his side, Darcy's fists clenched almost involuntarily. "Respectfully, I disagree," he said as calmly as he could.

Mr Bennet stared upwards a moment and heaved a sigh before saying, "Ah, but it is, for you see, the ladies have gone to Gunter's. Elizabeth is very fond of the pistachio cream ices."

CHAPTER EIGHT

The treats at Gunter's were delightful, but Elizabeth could not rouse her customary enthusiasm for her favourite, the *neige de pistachio*. Her father had insisted they all leave the house and treat themselves on this, their last day in London. Elizabeth would never have agreed to it, save for an unreasonable and silly hope that by entering the streets close to him, she might somehow encounter Mr Darcy.

Mr Gardiner had of late indulged himself in a new landau, capacious and elegant, the very place to revel in both the open air and the ices on a warm spring afternoon. The ladies appreciated the treat to varying degrees —Mrs Gardiner enjoying it fully, Jane determinedly, and Elizabeth half-heartedly.

"I think if you have finished pushing your dessert around with the spoon, Lizzy, we ought to return home,"

Mrs Gardiner said at last. "The children will be wondering where we went, but we must not tell, for they will be disappointed we did not take them."

"Next time," said Jane brightly. "I shall take them all."

Following the visit of Mr Darcy and his group to Gracechurch Street, Jane had decided it was time to put Mr Bingley and the misery associated with him aside. She had since donned at least the appearance of good spirits and had even forced herself to return a shy smile to a gentleman who tipped his hat at her while the ladies enjoyed their treats.

It came to nothing, of course, and was a small thing, but Elizabeth was proud of her sister for doing even that much. *Every journey begins as a small step*, she mused, then wondered if her own steps would take her on a journey towards or away from Mr Darcy.

The carriage began to move, and with one last sigh, Elizabeth looked out towards the square. A sound behind her caught her notice—almost as if someone were calling her name—but she thought it could not be and paid no heed.

The call was repeated a second time. "Mrs Gardiner! Halloo there!"

A third time, it came with authority. "You there! Stop the carriage!"

By then, Elizabeth had twisted in her seat to see if it

was who she imagined—wished—it might be. Her heart immediately began to flutter when she saw him.

Mr Darcy, breathless, with his coat and hat askew, had just gained upon them as the carriage stopped moving. "Good man," Elizabeth heard him say to Mrs Gardiner's driver, "I shall delay you but a moment or two."

"Mr Darcy, will you not join us, sir? Perhaps we can take you somewhere?" said Mrs Gardiner as though it were a perfectly common occurrence to have a distinguished gentleman chase down their carriage.

"No, I thank you." His eyes had met Elizabeth's and did not waver. "I, um, wondered if I might speak to your niece. To Miss Elizabeth."

Elizabeth was already preparing to exit the carriage when Mrs Gardiner agreed. Mr Darcy waved to their driver to remain where he was and assisted her by lowering the step and handing her down. They moved a few feet away from the carriage.

"I saw Mr Bennet at my club, and he told me I might find you here."

"My father?" Elizabeth exclaimed, horror-struck at imagining how her father might have behaved. Satiric discourse was likely the best for which she could hope.

"We had an excellent conversation, he and I. It made me realise I had more I wished to say to you than I spoke previously."

Elizabeth opened her mouth, wanting to know more

but then glanced back at the carriage. Jane and her aunt hastily looked away in a manner that let Elizabeth know they had been staring.

Mr Darcy also saw it and said, "I wonder if I might see you back to Gracechurch Street."

Elizabeth glanced around. Being that he had clearly run some distance to meet them, she assumed his carriage was not with him, and a cursory glance confirmed it. "On foot?" she asked.

He inclined his head very briefly. "It is three miles, but unless you are much altered since last autumn, I know you capable of it."

She smiled faintly and called out to Mrs Gardiner. "Aunt, Mr Darcy wishes to return me to Gracechurch Street on foot. Have you any objection?"

"We will not tarry, madam," Mr Darcy added.

Mrs Gardiner granted her permission and then instructed her driver to continue on their way. Elizabeth waved to them and saw Jane move over to take the place where she had been sitting next to their aunt. Immediately, they both bent their heads towards one another.

Goodness, at least let me be out of earshot before you start gossiping about me, she thought in fond remonstrance.

Turning her attention to Mr Darcy, Elizabeth noticed his gaze was upon her. Feeling shy, she fell back on that which had never failed her: her ability to tease.

"I am told that walking in London, save for the park, is not fashionable."

"I have lately learnt," said Mr Darcy, "that excessive worry over what others might think is a sure receipt for misery."

"Then by all means, let us walk."

There was so much to say that neither could speak for a moment, and when they did, both spoke at once.

"How does your—"

"Your father said—"

Both stopped, laughed, and Mr Darcy cleared his throat. "You first, please."

"I only meant to ask after your sister. I so enjoyed meeting her."

"It was her very great pleasure to meet you," he said. "She will be vastly disappointed to learn she is not to see you this summer at Pemberley."

She gave him a quick glance. "I see my father has spoken to you of his strictures?" When he nodded, Elizabeth continued. "He is not best pleased with me. He seemed to imagine that being in London taught me to value wealth over character and thought to keep me home to protect me from my own frailties."

"I know you too well to think that is true."

"It is not," Elizabeth agreed softly. "In fact, what I said was this: should I find that Pemberley was no more than a ramshackle peasant cottage, it could not alter my opinion of its master one bit."

He stopped walking for a moment, and she did as well. "I was exceedingly happy to learn in the park the other day that your opinions had changed. Yet, I was happier still to learn today that I might perhaps have hope?"

She inhaled sharply, and suddenly, her chest felt tight. A quick peep at him showed he, too, appeared affected, though he continued speaking.

"I do not expect to find your feelings so very changed on the strength of a walk and a call, but your father said you refused to promise *not* to consider me. If the converse is true—that you might one day consider me—pray tell me so at once. I could not bear to deceive myself over what your father indicated may be nothing more than a determination to carry your point."

His last remark made her laugh lightly. "Even *I* am not so obstinate as to forgo a holiday to prove a point."

"Then...may I hope?"

Again she beheld his countenance, this time looking at her with such tenderness that it quite discomposed her. "You may," she said quietly.

CHAPTER NINE

I t took them a great deal of time to traverse the miles from Berkeley Square to Gracechurch Street, yet somehow the time flew by. Elizabeth could scarcely credit how close to the dinner hour it was when at last they arrived on her aunt's doorstep.

They found the family awaiting them in the saloon, Jane, Mr Bennet and Mr and Mrs Gardiner all together. Mr Bennet was mostly silent while Mrs Gardiner fussed over how tired they must be from walking such a distance and invited Mr Darcy to stay and dine with them.

"Oh, Aunt, um," Elizabeth exclaimed, feeling herself flush, "no doubt Mr Darcy has many demands—"

"I would absolutely love nothing more," said Mr Darcy firmly. "Thank you, madam. You are too kind."

Mrs Gardiner seemed pleased, then directed her

attention to a conversation between Mr Bennet and her husband.

Elizabeth turned towards Mr Darcy on the sofa where they had both taken a seat. "Sir, you are too good. I fear this dinner plan is not pleasing to you, and I assure you, should you wish to make an excuse—"

"Make an excuse! Not a bit," he said in such accents that she could not doubt the veracity of his words. "I am very pleased with your aunt's kindness."

"I did not think you much enjoyed your last visit here," she said, still speaking quietly.

"What I did not enjoy was my relations and their outlandish and perhaps offending behaviour. We were like a band of Gypsies. If I was not ashamed of myself before for saying..."

He glanced towards the others across the room. Lowering his voice further, he continued. "For what I said before. I am heartily ashamed of myself now. To speak to the woman I love in such a way! And how absurd to task you for the actions of your relations when surely mine are nothing of which to boast. I never knew I was such a hypocrite."

"Perhaps we ought to make a vow," Elizabeth said lightly, "that I shall not hold the behaviour of your relations against you, if you will not hold mine against me."

"The first of many vows, I hope," he said with a look that made her feel liquid inside. After a quick glance about him, he brushed the back of her hand with his fingertips. It was all she could do to refrain from shivering.

It was a fine dinner. Even Mr Bennet was in agreeable spirits, with none of his earlier recalcitrance. Elizabeth enjoyed it even as she was distracted by the gentleman on her right side. How greatly her feelings for Mr Darcy had altered and in so short a time!

Yet, one substantial problem remained. His friend no longer had a house in Hertfordshire, and she had forsworn her northern tour with her aunt and uncle. Surely, when her father saw her genuine attachment to Mr Darcy, he would—no. It would not do. If anything, Mr Bennet would likely find satiric delight in tormenting her once he knew she was in earnest.

What future had she with Mr Darcy if she had no hope of future meetings with him?

In the end, it had been Mr Darcy who handily solved the problem of her travel to Derbyshire.

Having prevailed upon Mr Bingley for the use of Netherfield for the remaining weeks of his lease, Mr Darcy soon became a regular caller at Longbourn. Things did not begin in a promising way. Mrs Bennet's reaction when she realised Mr Darcy was there for Elizabeth was deeply mortifying. She soon learnt to hurry him into her father's study when he arrived, and he seemed appreciative of her efforts. He and Mr Bennet had played chess together after dinner at the Gardiners' home and rapidly discovered in each other a worthy opponent both in chess and in debate.

"What is this, Darcy?" Mr Bennet grumbled after his first loss. "Do you think if you defeat me often enough, I will change my mind about sending Elizabeth with her aunt and uncle?"

"Not at all, sir. I am perfectly content to woo her within her own neighbourhood," said Mr Darcy smoothly. "After all, you can hardly imagine Miss Elizabeth confused by my wealth or by Pemberley when she is being courted in the surroundings of her own home."

And woo her he did, with long rambles through the Hertfordshire countryside, family dinners, and even assemblies where the neighbourhood quickly learnt to revise their opinion of him.

"I always thought he had an eye for her," Mrs Long told Mrs Bennet.

"As did I," her mother squawked indignantly in reply. "But do you think that girl listens to a thing I say? She would be married by now if she had!"

But the means by which Mr Darcy ensured Elizabeth's travel to Pemberley was begun perfectly innocently. He was with Elizabeth, Jane, and Mrs Bennet in the cutting garden when Lydia ran up to them all and excitedly announced her plan to go to Brighton to follow the officers. Mrs Bennet, just as excitedly, voiced her support of the scheme.

Mr Darcy just then glanced at Elizabeth and she, in turn, silently implored him to help. Almost immediately he silently set the basket he had been holding for the ladies onto the ground. Then he excused himself and went to—Elizabeth later learnt—Mr Bennet's study, wherein he explained to him why he must not, under any circumstances, allow his youngest daughter to go off to Brighton. Mr Darcy told Elizabeth's father in plain terms why certain militia members were never to be trusted, and Mr Bennet had responded as he ought. Lydia's plans were rapidly denounced.

As a result, none of them at Longbourn had a moment's peace. Lydia was determined to make them all suffer for her deprivation.

"Pemberley is a quiet place," Mr Darcy informed Mr Bennet as they stood one afternoon in June watching Elizabeth, Jane, and Kitty play Coronella, a game Mr Darcy had brought down from London.

"Is it, hmm?" Mr Bennet asked while Elizabeth pricked up her ears to listen. "I envy you that, sir, likely more than anything else."

"The library there is the work of many generations," said Mr Darcy idly, almost as though the thought had only just occurred to him. "I confess I do not even know how many books are there. I surely have not read them all."

Elizabeth chanced a peek at her father but turned her attention back to the game. Kitty had learnt it the fastest and was proving a worthy opponent.

"The library is towards the back of the house which has excellent light most of the day and is out of the way of the servants and their business."

"What is it to me how quiet and grand is the library at Pemberley?" Mr Bennet asked, a little bitterly.

"I was only thinking," said Mr Darcy, offering a little clap to Elizabeth who had just caught a particularly difficult toss, "that this promise Miss Elizabeth made you. It was that she would give up travel with her aunt and uncle, yes?"

Elizabeth peeped over her shoulder in time to see Mr Bennet incline his head.

"Then if she came to Pemberley with *you*, sir, her promise to you would remain inviolate and you would have the benefit of a peaceful sojourn in Derbyshire, ensuring Elizabeth did not lose her head."

Elizabeth is not going to lose her head, Elizabeth thought. *Though her heart is another matter entirely.*

"Are you inviting me to Pemberley, Darcy?" Mr Bennet sounded amused by the notion, but Elizabeth did not dare turn to look at him.

"In the spirit of full disclosure, I am inviting you to bring your daughter to Pemberley."

Mr Bennet chuckled, after which there was a silence. Elizabeth fervently hoped her father was contemplating the myriad ways in which his peace was cut up at Longbourn presently: the daily weeping and raging against the unfairness of life to which Lydia subjected them all, Kitty's arguments with Lydia over whose life had a greater share of injustice, or Mary and her efforts to learn to play the harp lute. They could hear the discordant twangs even from their present distance from the house.

"I daresay it is not the worst idea I have heard," Mr Bennet finally pronounced and then excused himself to return to his study.

As soon as he was gone, Elizabeth nearly skipped to Mr Darcy's side. Squeezing his hand, she said, "You, sir, are a genius."

He tapped her lightly on her nose. "You inspire me."

CHAPTER TEN

From her very first sight of it, Pemberley delighted Elizabeth. She tried not to gasp but failed, and her father, seated across from her in the carriage, looked up from his newspaper and frowned.

She shook her head at him. "Surely, after all these weeks you cannot still believe I am only interested in Mr Darcy's wealth?"

Mr Bennet folded the newspaper and set it to his side. "I shall grant you that the Mr Darcy we saw this summer in Hertfordshire is a far different fellow than the man we met last autumn."

"And now that you are in full understanding of what happened to him just before coming to Netherfield, do you not understand why he might have been in dampened spirits?"

"You refer to the matter of his sister?" Mr Bennet asked. On Elizabeth's nod, he continued. "Yes, that is true, but my girl, you must know that Mr Darcy will never be of the disposition that overflows in mirth."

"Perhaps not but I do think the right wife will enliven him."

"He will never be at ease amongst those he considers inferior to him."

"He is not much at ease with anyone," Elizabeth replied. "His idea of good company is a few close friends and a quiet evening."

"And *your* philosophy is that one can never have too large a party."

"A difference, that is true, but if everyone married someone exactly like themselves, how dull their lives would be!"

"In other words, you are determined to have him," Mr Bennet said, peering at her over the top of his spectacles.

She had not before thought of it in such definite terms. Yes, the understanding that she had been falling in love with him had been creeping up upon her since that fateful day in Hyde Park. In the time since, she had come to understand that in their talents and disposi-tions, they exactly suited one another more than she ever could have imagined.

But love could not be reduced to such terms as that.

Love was not some balance-sheet of debits and credits, whereupon the advantages of one were weighed against the disadvantages of the other. Love was the fact that she wished, above all things, to be with Mr Darcy always. Love was feeling completed in him, knowing she could be her best self with him, and he his best self with her.

She did not need to confide that much to her father, however, certainly not when she had never even confessed her feelings to Mr Darcy himself. So, in answer she said merely, "Yes, Papa, in fact, I *am* determined to have him."

Mr Bennet smiled blandly and looked out the window. They had just drawn up to the portico of the grand limestone edifice. "Well, we had better go in then."

A large party was on hand to receive the two travellers from Hertfordshire. Jane and the Gardiners had arrived at Pemberley earlier in the day. Lord Saye was there with one of his friends, a Sir Frederick Moore, who seemed already to have fallen under Jane's spell—and she under his. Elizabeth resolved to ask about *that* later. Miss Darcy was a nervous but determined hostess, and Elizabeth congratulated her on an excellent job seeing to all of their comforts.

Only one person did not seem light-hearted and gay, and that was Darcy himself. His smile was a trifle forced, and his complexion was pale. Elizabeth worried about him as the group sat and partook of a hearty array of meats, breads, and fruit in Pemberley's largest drawing room, all the while regaling one another with tales of their travels.

"Jane," she whispered to her sister as she came near. When Jane looked over, Elizabeth mouthed, "Sir Frederick?"

Jane came closer. "You will recall that day when we ate ices at Gunter's?"

The timing of her explanation was unfortunate, as Lord Saye had only just come to take a some fruit from the table behind them and chose to join their conversation.

"You know—the same day that Darcy went tearing through the square like a great galloping gollompus and terrified all the children." He laughed heartily at his own joke and strolled away.

Darcy, seated on a sofa nearby with Mr Gardiner only rolled his eyes at the insult and picked at something on his plate.

Elizabeth turned back to her sister. "I remember. You met him then? Was it after I walked off?"

"We had noticed one another beforehand," Jane said, furiously blushing. "But then, we were stopped on the other side of the square, and he was as well, and we spoke a little bit. I am sure it is all nothing, but he is a very kind gentleman."

He looked kind, though not exceedingly handsome—short and seemed to be balding or about to—but decidedly good-humoured. Who knew what, if anything, would come of it, but Elizabeth was glad to see her sister enjoying the first blush of romance.

Darcy rose then and came to kneel beside her. "When you have rested, would you like to take a walk?"

"Very much," she said with a smile. "And I do not need to rest. Stretching my legs will do me much better, I think."

It was not long before they were strolling amongst beautiful blossoms on one of Pemberley's pretty paths. *Everything about Pemberley is exquisite*, Elizabeth thought. *Elegance without ostentation or artifice*

"Do you remember," he began, "that night in the parsonage?"

"The night you proposed?"

Darcy grimaced. "In a manner of speaking. I suppose I should hope you do *not* remember it."

She laughed but knew not how else to reply.

"That night, I begged you to relieve my suffering and consent to be my wife. I must confess though at that time—" He shook his head. "At that time, I had no notion of real suffering. Real suffering was your refusal. Real suffering was reconciliation without knowing what might await us. Real suffering was falling more deeply in love with you than I had ever imagined possible and then being forced to be apart."

She squeezed his arm gently. "It has only been a fort-night, though I confess it has felt much longer to me too."

"Only a fortnight—yet, I have been the most wretched creature I could ever imagine! Dearest, loveli-est, Elizabeth! What you have done to me, I shall never know, but all I do know is that my house no longer feels like a home without you in it. Pemberley is desperate for you...*I* am desperate for you. You belong with me, Eliza-beth. I have never been more certain of that than I am now," he said in a rush.

She looked up at him. "As am I."

He seemed as if he had been prepared to say more, but her words stopped him. He exhaled, his dark gaze never leaving her countenance. "You are what?"

"Certain that...I belong with you." Suddenly shy, she dropped her gaze, but he would not have it. Reaching for her chin with one finger, he tenderly moved it back to him.

"Of all the things I said to you that night in Hunsford parsonage," he said taking her hands in his own, "there is only one other thing that bears repeating, and that is that I ardently admire and love you. It is my dearest wish that you would marry me."

"I would be very honoured, sir," she said softly.

He brought her hands to his lips for a soft kiss, saying in a whisper, "You are too good for me, and I intend to spend the rest of my days seeking to be worthy of you."

She had no idea what to say, but in the end, it did not signify—for her lips were soon more agreeably engaged.

The End

ALSO BY AMY D'ORAZIO

A Fine Joke

A Folly of Youth

A Match Made at Matlock

A Lady's Reputation

A Short Period of Exquisite Felicity

A Wilful Misunderstanding

Heart Enough

Of a Sunday Evening

So Material a Change

The Best Part of Love

The Happiest Couple in the World

The Mysteries of Pemberley

Wits & Wagers

SHORT STORY ANTHOLOGIES

An Inducement into Matrimony

'Tis the Season: Variations on a Jane Austen Christmas

Happily Ever After with Mr Darcy

ABOUT THE AUTHOR

Amy D'Orazio is a longtime devotee of Jane Austen and fiction related to her characters. She began writing her own little stories to amuse herself during hours spent at sports practices and the like and soon discovered a passion for it. By far, however, the thing she loves most is the connections she has made with readers and other writers of Austenesque fiction.

Amy currently lives in Myrtle Beach with her husband and daughters, as well as three Jack Russell terriers who often make appearances (in a human form) in her books.

For the latest information on new releases and sales please follow Amy on Bookbub or her Amazon Author Page.

INSUFFICIENT VANITY

LM ROMANO

But it was a hope shortly checked by other considerations, and she soon felt that even her vanity was insufficient, when required to depend upon his affection for her–for a woman who had already refused him–as able to overcome a sentiment so natural as abhorrence against relationship with Wickham.

— PRIDE & PREJUDICE, CHAPTER 52

CHAPTER ONE

※━━━━━━━━━※

September 1812, Longbourn

C*runch!* The papers she clutched crackled loudly, disturbing the quiet peace of her hiding place amongst the trees.

Cursing her unseemly haste, Elizabeth Bennet released a blessedly inaudible sigh as she loosened her hold on the correspondence gripped within her palm. If she was not careful, the charming refuge she had found for herself would soon be discovered—and all for a want of patience. Perhaps she ought not to have brought such a temptation with her, for indeed, what she most desired was to swiftly devour every word her aunt had written. *Oh, why must stationery make such noise!*

If only she had not been reduced to hiding in the first place. Yet, as her father often quoted, *"For extreme diseases, extreme methods of cure are most suitable."* Elizabeth inwardly sniggered at her father's probable amusement in likening George Wickham, her lamentably irksome brother-in-law, to a serious affliction described by an ancient Greek physician. Would that she could rid herself of the man as easily as lancing a boil! The process would probably be less painful by comparison.

*Thud...thud...thud...*Fallen leaves amplified the steps of a man's heavy boots on the ground. *Speak of the devil, and he shall appear.* Holding herself absolutely still, barely daring to draw breath, Elizabeth waited patiently to hear the longed-for retreat, cursing once again the dogged persistence of the infuriating man! Why would he not simply leave her alone?

"Miss Elizabeth."

He could not have spotted her yet, for she had chosen her present location in Longbourn's pretty little wilderness quite carefully. Sitting with her back resting against a wide tree trunk, flowering bushes sheltering her little copse on all sides, Elizabeth dared not move a muscle. Hearing her name called once more, she silently cursed the day she first saw the man walking down the street in Meryton. An unassuming man, a more reasonable man, would know beyond doubt that their previously friendly acquaintance was at an end, but George Wickham was not a reasonable man.

A rustling of foliage distracted Elizabeth from her practiced immobility, nearly startling her into a shriek.

Without warning, the fluffy, matted, orange fur tail of Longbourn's old barn cat brushed against her face. Bracing herself against the inevitable sneeze, Elizabeth nearly cried with relief when the man's footsteps faded away. She was safe—at least for a time. Unfortunately, it was a temporary pardon at best.

How had it come to this?

Though she had anticipated no pleasure in welcoming her sister Lydia and her husband to Longbourn after their scandalous elopement, Elizabeth was yet surprised by the sheer misery their visit had already brought. Since their arrival, the Wickhams had presented a rather cloying picture of newly wedded bliss to the family, though Elizabeth could well detect the insincerity underneath Mr Wickham's affected smiles. He had attempted, on numerous occasions and with a persistence that was maddening, to engage his new sister in more private conversation, no doubt hoping to rekindle their previous rapport. Elizabeth, however, could not bear the prospect of appearing on remotely cordial terms with the man, angry as she was over his previous deception regarding Mr Darcy's character and the heinous manner in which he had jeopardised the future of her entire family through her silliest sister.

Daring to return to the missive she held in her hand, Elizabeth let the truth of her aunt's words wash over her as she finished the final page. Aunt Gardiner had replied as fast as she possibly could to Elizabeth's request for information on Lydia's wedding, or more importantly, for information on its rather unlikely guest, Mr Darcy.

When she had foolishly disclosed the details of her sister's elopement to him at the inn in Lambton, Elizabeth had never expected Mr Darcy would take it upon himself to save her family's reputation. Indeed, she had only thought about what she had lost. A poor, country gentlewoman was already a most inadvisable choice of wife for a gentleman of Mr Darcy's wealth and station, but a *ruined*, poor, country gentlewoman was an impossible one. At the moment of his departure, she had surprised even herself with the acute longing and anguish that pervaded her being, knowing beyond doubt that he was indeed the best of men, and he was lost to her forever.

The sound of heavy footsteps on the path once again alerted Elizabeth to the approach of her nefarious brother-in-law. Unwilling to endure his presence, and requiring a better refuge, Elizabeth stood and walked at a brisk pace towards the orchards. She could not avoid Mr Wickham indefinitely but felt unequal to the task of exchanging pleasantries, much less endure his particular brand of flirtation.

The sheer impudence of the man! Who else would be so bold as to leer at his new sister under the dubious guise of gentlemanly charm?

Perhaps if her feelings were under better regulation, she could confront him in some subtle manner regarding the many falsehoods with which he had filled her mind during his previous sojourn in Hertfordshire. Indeed, it would be most thrilling to watch him writhe with the understanding that not only did she fully comprehend his previous deeds, but her knowledge also extended to precisely *who* had paid his debts and brought about his position as her brother. Her changed opinion on Mr Darcy would no doubt wound Mr Wickham's vanity, a momentarily cheering prospect, before the very same thought plunged her once again into despair. What did it matter if he knew she thought him a scoundrel and Mr Darcy an honourable gentleman?

Mr Darcy would never come to know her changed opinion of him, and even if he did, Elizabeth was absolutely certain that he could never bear to offer for her again, not if connexion to her family came with a brother whom he had every reason to loathe for all eternity. He could not love her so well as that—nor in her opinion, should he. In her own mind, her abuse of his character coupled with her defence of a rogue made her decidedly unworthy of his regard. Thankful for the private nature of her disappointment, Elizabeth reflected on how her father would indeed laugh at her misfortune, for she was more than a little crossed in love, though she did not find it as agreeable an experience as he had seemed to imply.

"Miss Elizabeth!"

A breathless shout recalled Elizabeth to her

surroundings, and she was startled to realise that Mr Wickham had discovered her, apparently intent upon staging an ambush. She froze, caught between an urge to run and her own mounting fury, sick to death of his unrelenting, miserable pursuit.

What he had evidently failed to notice, however, was that his wife was not far behind. Elizabeth watched her sister in dismay as Lydia's scowling expression shifted rapidly to shock as she lost her footing and stumbled over a tree root, crying out in pain as she toppled to the leaf-strewn ground.

"George! My—my ankle!"

As Lydia began to wail in earnest, Elizabeth ignored Mr Wickham's presence and rushed to her sister's side.

"Do you think you can walk, Liddy? What on earth possessed you to run through the trees in your house slippers?"

Tears streaming down her cheeks, Lydia petulantly replied, "I only...wished to...draw my husband's attention! You cannot...always have it for your own!"

With tremendous effort, Elizabeth refrained from lashing out at her sister's ridiculousness while her ne'er-do-well husband finally offered his services.

"Well now, my love. I suppose I ought to bring you into the house." Scooping Lydia into his arms, his young wife began to berate him over his inattention.

"I called out to you, George! Why did you not heed me? And why did you not...catch me?" Lydia sniffled.

As the Wickhams engaged in a heated conversation, littered with laments and accusations on Lydia's side and filled with soothing flattery on the part of Mr Wickham, Elizabeth veered off towards the stables to send a groom to Meryton for Mr Jones. Though Elizabeth doubted the injury was serious, she knew full well that Lydia would never be appeased until the apothecary had at least been consulted.

Upon entering the vestibule at Longbourn, Elizabeth was dismayed to find that Lydia's howls of pain had been joined by the shrill cries of her mother, who was clearly distraught over her youngest daughter's suffering.

"Oh my dear, sweet Lydia! How could you possibly be so clumsy, child!"

"But, Mama—"

"No, no, I cannot see you leaving for Newcastle now! Mr Bennet, you must insist that she stay until she is fully recovered!"

Alarmed by the prospect, especially over such a slight injury as a twisted ankle, Elizabeth was relieved to see her father had made an appearance amidst the chaos in the parlour.

"Calm yourself, Mrs Bennet. We do not know if her injury is so very grave." Locking eyes across the room, Elizabeth could see the relief on her father's face that someone with a more rational mind had arrived. "Lizzy dear, Lydia has told us you were there when she took a tumble. Where have you been?"

"I sent a groom into Meryton for Mr Jones, Papa."

"Ah. Very well, very well. See now, Mrs Bennet, we shall soon know the fate of our daughter's muddy foot."

As Lydia wailed afresh at her father's indelicate comment, Elizabeth decided to engage in more practical pursuits. After informing Mrs Hill of the apothecary's imminent arrival and the possible need for dressings to wrap her sister's foot and ankle, Elizabeth chose to wait outside for the man himself, hopeful at least that a little distance from both her sister's cries and her sister's husband would settle her spirits. It was not long before Jane found her just beyond the front portico.

"So, as I understand from Mama, Lydia fell in the orchard. I had not realised she ventured out of doors, for the last I saw her, she was trimming a bonnet with Kitty."

Elizabeth sighed as she leant against her elder sister. "Oh Jane! You have caught me in the midst of some rather uncharitable thoughts. How I wish I possessed your even temper, for I cannot begin to imagine living with our youngest sister and her husband for any longer than we possibly must! Do you know that Mama is already insisting that the Wickhams stay beyond Wednesday?"

With polite admonishment, Jane responded, "You know as well as I that if Lydia is truly injured, she should not travel so soon. If it is a slight injury, then it is likely she will be well in a day or two, which should not affect their plans to travel north."

"Well, here comes Mr Jones. Let us pray for a favourable report!"

"Lizzy, you are terrible!" Jane scolded, though Elizabeth could see that she was amused.

Easy enough for Jane to dismiss the seriousness of such a proposal. Wickham does not single her out as he does me. Nor does he seem to forget his manners in her presence.

"Good afternoon, Miss Bennet, Miss Elizabeth!"

"Good day to you, sir," Elizabeth replied, "Thank you for coming so quickly. Our sister, Mrs Wickham, tripped in the orchard and injured her ankle."

"Ah, I see! Well, take me to her, and I shall see what I can do."

Only a quarter of an hour later, Elizabeth learnt that fortune had as good as abandoned her, for not only did Mr Jones determine that Lydia suffered from a badly sprained ankle, but he also advised her against travel for at least a fortnight, possibly longer. With Mr Bennet's reluctant permission, Mr Wickham was all too eager to write to his commanding officer about the delay in their travels, something that failed to surprise Elizabeth. She was convinced he would seize any opportunity to avoid taking up his duties in the regulars, ungrateful louse that he was.

What wretched luck! Wickham, always nearby, seeming to lie in wait for me—now for another endless fortnight. Is it only my misery over what I have lost that makes every moment in his presence unendurable? Or is he hounding me on purpose? And either way, how will I bear it?

As she climbed into bed later that evening, Elizabeth was confident the coming weeks at her family home were sure to be the most intolerable of her life.

CHAPTER TWO

❧━━━❧

A s the noise of busy London streets faded into the distance, the insistent tapping of leather boots upon the floor of the carriage grew louder, calling attention to the obvious anxiety of one of the fine conveyance's occupants. While irritation would have been his natural response, as Fitzwilliam Darcy took in the nervous demeanour of his dear friend, he could only feel guilt at the role he had played in the present circumstances.

"Bingley, you will wear yourself out before we reach St Albans. I can loan you a book if it will help settle your mind."

As his ordinarily unruffled friend raked a nervous hand through his blond locks, he replied, "I could never quite master reading in a moving carriage. Though I suppose I have yet to master the art while seated in my own library."

"I shall not venture a response to that statement."

With a slight chuckle, Charles Bingley responded, "I appreciate that, and I apologise for my distraction. I still cannot believe that I may see my angel as soon as tomorrow, yet—yet I cannot help but believe that my return will be unwelcome. It was not very gallant of me to simply abandon the area last autumn without taking proper leave of my neighbours. She would be well-justified in hating me for my callous actions."

"A fault that ought to be counted as mine," Darcy uttered softly with true remorse.

"Yes, well, I believe it matters little now." With a slight shrug of his shoulders, Bingley turned his attention to the changing landscape beyond the carriage window, leaving Darcy alone with his thoughts.

Once again, the crushing weight of his past mistakes consumed Darcy's thinking. It had taken him months since his devastating disappointment in Hunsford to confess his deception to his friend regarding the matter of Miss Jane Bennet. Bingley had been by turns shocked and angered at Darcy's presumption, though to his credit, he acknowledged his own error in deferring so completely to another's opinion. At least Bingley had accepted that Darcy had never meant to injure him or the lady, but rather sought to protect his friend through his misguided actions. Bingley's sisters, however, were not granted the same reprieve. Miss Bingley and Mrs Hurst thought nothing of their brother's wounded heart, nor what their actions had wrought upon the kind and gentle Miss Bennet. Together, they simply wished to further their own social ambitions through a much loftier marriage for their brother, ambitions that would not be satisfied by an unknown and practically penniless country squire's daughter.

One thing for which Darcy was eternally grateful was the absence of Miss Bingley in his Hertfordshire-bound coach. When his friend resolved to return to his leased estate of Netherfield Park, he requested Darcy's presence, but only if he would fully support his efforts to woo and marry Miss Bennet. As her opposition to the marriage was well known, Miss Bingley was not granted a similar invitation.

"Pray excuse me for asking, but I wonder—how *did* your sister react to your plans to return to Netherfield?"

At his question, Bingley coloured and tugged at his cravat. "Well, that is, I-I am not sure...well, dash it all, Darcy, I simply do not know!"

"I do not take your meaning. How could you possibly not know?"

"I was so impatient to begin our journey that I simply quit my rooms at The Albany and had my man send over my effects to Darcy House. I did stop at the Hursts' home to leave a note, but I confess I did not wait for a response, nor was I certain that my sisters were in residence."

"You left a note?" Darcy's incredulous tone brought a sheepish look to Bingley's visage.

"Very well, my courage escaped me! To be quite frank, I am still extremely vexed by my sister's false friendship towards Miss Bennet and her terrible actions against me. I knew she would vent her spleen upon me the minute she discovered my purpose in returning, and I simply wished to spare myself her vitriol."

"You *do* realise that after reading your missive, Miss Bingley may take it upon herself to travel to Hertford-shire and foil your plans," Darcy pointed out, uneasy with the likelihood of Miss Bingley's appearance and how it might disrupt his own intentions for their stay near Meryton. Intentions that Darcy had not yet relayed even to Bingley, so closely did he hold them to his heart.

"My sister and the Hursts were invited to a house party in Sussex—some old family friend of Hurst's father. Last I knew, they were to leave in a se'nnight. I believe the heir to the estate is unwed, and Louisa has great plans for Caroline during their stay. It is about time my sister married, and I think that after our stay at Pemberley this past summer she has finally given up her designs on you."

Darcy could not fully share Bingley's optimism about his sister's hopes. While it would relieve him greatly if the lady chose to divert her attentions elsewhere, he did not believe she would resign herself so easily to her brother's prospective bride.

"I can only hope you are correct in this instance, for I do not believe your sister would aid your efforts to win Miss Bennet, as her disdain for some of the ladies at Longbourn was quite well-marked."

"Ah yes, Miss Elizabeth. Caroline was quite put out by the lady's presence in Derbyshire, though I must say, I have always enjoyed Miss Elizabeth's lively manners and how she so skilfully deflects Caroline's remarks with kindness. She even seemed to get on well with you, if I recall, with none of those debates you always seemed to start at Netherfield."

"Yes, she is truly an estimable woman."

Darcy felt discomfited by Bingley's recollections, as he did not wish to ruminate on Elizabeth's past antipathy towards him.

Elizabeth.

If only Bingley knew the true reason he had so readily consented to return to Hertfordshire. While he had every intention of supporting his friend, Darcy's true purpose was to see *her* again, and to ascertain if she could ever hold him in tender regard—to see if she could come to love him as ardently as he loved her.

Surprised and delighted by her presence in Derbyshire over the summer, Darcy was certain he had detected a softening in her manner towards him. He had even begun to hope that she might possibly accept him before she quit Lambton, but all of his desires had come crashing down with one fateful letter. Recalling the pain and anguish he felt at her tears over her sister's ill-considered elopement, Darcy knew he would feel infinitely worse were she to discover his role in her sister's patched up marriage.

He could not bear to receive her gratitude, and truly, such feelings would be misguided at best. *Gratitude?* For saving her family's reputation by tying them forever to the most loathsome man of his acquaintance? If only her sister had been willing to leave Wickham behind when he discovered the pair in London, he could have found a more suitable match. Of this Darcy was certain.

What was I thinking? Surely, she must have suffered through the Wickhams' visit to Longbourn. The only consolation she most likely experienced was the brevity of the encounter! How could I, who knows better than most, expose Elizabeth to the mortification that close affiliation to Wickham affords?

Perhaps I should not underestimate her resilience, though she withstood my boorish behaviour at Netherfield and Rosings without even betraying a hint of her dislike. She has probably skewered her new brother with her keen wit a hundred times over —and all with a beautiful smile and twinkling eyes. I could travel the world and never find her equal. She is worth anything and everything—sister to Wickham be damned! But will she want me?

Darcy had carefully timed their arrival in the neighbourhood for after the Wickhams' departure for Newcastle, fully aware that he would not be able to present himself at his best if he were forced to share the newly married couple's company. He also sincerely doubted young Mrs Wickham's ability to keep his actions regarding their marriage a secret, since the lady had ably demonstrated that discretion was not an attribute she possessed. Darcy hoped that a few days would be enough to restore Elizabeth's equanimity after the Wickhams' removal and, more importantly, that Bingley's renewed attentions towards her dearest sister would please her. He fervently wished to secure her happiness in all things, and just maybe, he himself would feature in her greater contentment.

The sharp, incessant tapping of fingertips on the opposite windowpane drew Darcy's attention once again to his nervous friend. So many hopes were wrapped up in this one visit, and despite his own feelings of trepidation, Darcy felt that genuine felicity for Bingley and himself could quite possibly be within reach.

CHAPTER THREE

"A little to the left, Lizzy! Have you no pity for my poor ankle?"

Gritting her teeth, Elizabeth shifted her mother's ruffled pillow a small measure to the left, all under the watchful gaze of an impatient Lydia.

"There. I trust you are finally comfortable."

Petulantly, Lydia replied, "As comfortable as I can be, I suppose. But now I think I would rather like another cup of tea. You will fetch one for me, will you not? You know how I like it."

"I daresay we *all* know your preferences. Did I not bring you a fresh cup but five minutes ago?"

"Well yes, but it is too cold for me now. Ring the bell for Hill, Lizzy. The pot is obviously not warm enough! A good hostess would know the difference, surely."

Bristling at the slight, Elizabeth checked the still

warm teapot before turning back to face her irritating sister.

"And where is your husband, Liddy? Should *he* not be directing the servants and seeing to your comfort?"

Glaring at Elizabeth, Lydia opened her mouth to retort but was interrupted by their mother.

"Oh, stop fussing, Lizzy, and ring for Hill! I am sure Mr Wickham is occupied with more important matters, silly girl!"

"Yes, Mama," Elizabeth replied with a sigh. If she did not escape the house soon, her reserve of patience would be well and truly spent.

"I can sort the tea. Why do you not go for a walk?" Jane gently suggested.

"It does not matter which of my sisters prepares my drink, for since they are all still *single*, they can have nothing better to do," Lydia commented, smiling as she preened once again about her married state.

"God bless you, Jane!" Elizabeth murmured as she seized the opportunity to flee the parlour and venture out onto one of her favourite paths.

A short while later, as a rush of cool morning wind swept over the peak of Oakham Mount and down the gentle slopes into the valley below, Elizabeth could see that autumn had indeed come in earnest. Vibrant red and orange leaves rustled in the breeze like glittering jewels, reminding her once again why she favoured this particular season. It was one of change and of new opportunities. If only nature's brilliant display would herald a similar alteration in her own circumstances, for Elizabeth was not entirely sure she could endure another evening at Longbourn like those of the last few days.

Why cannot Lydia simply hold her tongue? If I am forced to wait upon her one more time—or worse—to hear one more glowing speech about her scapegrace husband, I may well go mad!

Unfortunately, Lydia's many effusions were also filled with tales of her exploits in Brighton, prompting disgust in not only Elizabeth, but Jane, and Mary as well, though Jane was too polite to allow her disapproval to show. For once, Elizabeth did not resent Mary's tendency to spout moral homilies and scriptures in admonishment of Lydia's antics. Even though it was readily apparent that Lydia was beyond correction, or even beyond feeling guilt for her shameful behaviour, Elizabeth found it strangely satisfying that not every member of the Bennet family pretended approval for Lydia's reckless, though unfortunately necessary union.

Her mother's behaviour, though not quite under-standable, was entirely expected. All of the moaning and hysterical lamentations that had poured forth out of the mistress's chambers during the weeks of Lydia's disap-pearance had shifted promptly to outbursts of joy at the marriage of her youngest daughter. Mr Wickham had also achieved a rapid recovery in the eyes of Mrs Bennet, and far from being the worst scoundrel ever to enter

Meryton, he was lauded as the handsome and dashing son-in-law she had always desired.

In Elizabeth's opinion, her father's response was not altogether better. Though he knew the man to be completely worthless and dissolute, Mr Bennet encouraged Wickham's simpering smiles and vacuous compliments. He delighted in witnessing the man's buffoonery, knowing how little substance existed behind his pretence of charm. Recently however, her father's tendency to make sport of any situation only prompted Elizabeth's vexation, reminding her once again of the justness of Mr Darcy's opinions regarding her family.

Her father's lack of concern over Mr Wickham's presence at Longbourn also meant that Elizabeth's own recent struggles to evade the attentions of said gentleman had gone entirely unnoticed. As the head of the household, and indeed as a guiding hand to her younger sisters, Mr Bennet's open disapproval of his son-in-law's character could provide some protection, or at least have the happy effect of discouraging a similar alliance in her sister, Kitty. As it was, his lack of forthright criticism, no doubt engendered by his desire to avoid conflict with his wife and most vocal daughter, was slowly starting to strip away the gravity of Lydia's transgression in Kitty's eyes.

Though she was two years older, Kitty had always admired and followed Lydia's every move. So easy in company, so boisterous and relentlessly jolly, Lydia almost inspired awe in her somewhat insipid elder sister. Without Lydia, Kitty had been floundering under the combined disapproval of both of her parents and her inability to occupy her time in Lydia's absence. Elizabeth was almost pained for her sister as she began to realise just how completely Kitty had given way to their youngest sister in everything—her interests, her pastimes, even her conversation had been so thoroughly subsumed to the desires of another.

Kitty was truly the only Bennet sister who looked upon her brother-in-law with the same reverence that Lydia had desired from them all. To Kitty, her sister had been most fortunate to capture such a handsome redcoat for a husband. Elizabeth could only pray that she would not be given the same opportunity as Lydia to fall for a rake.

And then there was Jane, dear Jane, who despite her knowledge to the contrary, was somehow convinced that Mr Wickham's character was not completely lost to any and all reform. Elizabeth could scarcely credit Jane's belief in the happiness of Lydia's marriage, particularly when cracks had already begun to appear in their cheerful posturing only a few weeks into the couple's dubious state of wedded bliss.

The Bennet temper was well known in Longbourn. Elizabeth herself owned a fair share of this rather unfortunate quality that pervaded her father's side of the family tree, to which poor Mr Darcy could well attest.

While this rather passionate temperament had completely escaped some of her sisters, Jane being the most distant from this regrettable attribute, it was widely acknowledged that Lydia had inherited the lion's share, and sadly for Elizabeth, her youngest sister's temper had lately turned in her own direction.

It had apparently not escaped Lydia's notice that her husband repeatedly sought Elizabeth's company, and while Elizabeth used every method imaginable to discourage his attention, the only interpretation Lydia would entertain was that her sister must be jealous.

Jealous. The mere idea of envying Lydia's situation was enough to make Elizabeth's skin crawl. She had tried numerous times and with increasingly desperate measures to evade Mr Wickham's many attempts at conversation, yet the man's efforts continued unabated. What could he possibly hope to accomplish by so singling her out? Why on earth did he believe that she would be receptive to his overtures of friendship? Did he truly think her such a simpleton as to be unaware of the devastation he had nearly wrought on her entire family? The gall of her despicable new brother never failed to rile Elizabeth's own temper.

Does he not realise that should he succeed in commandeering my notice, he could very well be subject to my less than charitable thoughts? Evidently, his confidence in my ability to restrain my tongue is greater than mine own.

The cheerful song of birds pulled Elizabeth from her

troublesome thoughts, and as she looked out upon the beautiful, peaceful surroundings of Hertfordshire's glorious countryside, she was temporarily distracted in wondering whether or not Derbyshire had welcomed autumn in the same manner as her home. Did Mr Darcy look out upon a similar blanket of warm, colourful trees and fields, or did the peaks still retain the stunning greenery she had witnessed on her summer travels? Did he, too, sit upon a local promontory and take comfort in nature's soothing presence?

Does he long for me as I long for him?

Though wishing to chastise herself for the laughable direction of her musings, Elizabeth could not help but wish Mr Darcy would arrive and somehow rescue her from her current situation. With a weary heart, Elizabeth gathered her shawl and bonnet and began her long walk back to Longbourn.

As she meandered along the paths, she tried to reconcile her hopes with the disappointing reality she faced: Mr Darcy would not be returning to Hertfordshire, he would not continue to pursue a woman who had rejected him so vociferously, and he most certainly would never make a brother of Mr Wickham. As her anger began to rise once more towards the reprobate who was currently ensconced in her family home, Elizabeth's energetic strides turned into stomps as she attempted to release her ire before reaching her destination. All of her efforts, however, were in vain as the one person she least wished to see was waiting for her on the edge of Longbourn's park.

"Ah Sister! I was hoping to meet you upon your return. Enjoying the lovely weather, I take it?"

Dear Lord, why must I be forced to endure this man? At least the house is in sight!

Walking past Mr Wickham after the barest of nods in his direction, Elizabeth replied, "I am sure you are well aware, sir, that I usually partake of a long walk in the morning. I find it settles my spirits as nothing else quite can, particularly when I anticipate any number of challenges in my day."

"Challenges? Are you finding the company at Longbourn to be particularly trying of late? I must confess, I had quite feared that you no longer cared for me, though I know you could not truly wish for my absence."

"That is amusing, sir, for I believed that my disinclination for your presence was obvious." *Well, I suppose that was a tad uncivil.*

Mr Wickham's smug smile that had prompted Elizabeth's moment of uncharacteristic frankness was temporarily replaced by a tight expression of anger. He released a feigned and awkward chuckle as he regained his well-practiced charm and extended his arm to Elizabeth, though she continued to walk at a determined pace towards the house.

"Now, now, I insist that we have a most brotherly chat, for I fear there has been some misunderstanding between us that must be resolved ere your sister and I depart."

Relieved to see the door to the manor house in sight, Elizabeth responded in a cheerful tone. "Oh, I do not believe that to be necessary, Mr Wickham. After all, why should there be any misunderstandings between us? I thank you for your consideration, but I really must be going about my day."

A quick glance to the side revealed her new brother's continued anger at her easy dismissal. Her satisfaction at his discomfort, however, quickly turned to fear as he began to reach for her arm.

"Now truly, I must insist—"

Relief, overwhelming and entirely propitious relief, came from a most unexpected source. The sound of approaching riders halted Mr Wickham's quest for her arm, and a grateful Elizabeth turned a beaming smile towards her unwitting rescuers. Yet, gratitude rapidly shifted to surprise, when much to her astonishment, her gaze locked with the concerned eyes of none other than Mr Darcy.

CHAPTER FOUR

W itnessing the relief in the eyes of the woman he adored, Darcy had never experienced such a contrariety of emotions in all of his eight and twenty years of living. What the devil was the blackguard still doing in Hertfordshire? Why had his own arrival prompted a look of such profound consolation and gratitude on Elizabeth's beautiful face? Had Wickham been importuning her, his own sister-in-law?

Bingley dismounted upon their arrival and was in the midst of exchanging enthusiastic pleasantries with Elizabeth, though Darcy noted that even the jovial Bingley appeared to detect the tension between Mr Wickham and his new sister. When he finally succeeded in pulling his attention from Elizabeth's expressive features, anxiously ascertaining her welfare, Darcy dismounted and joined the somewhat awkward conversation.

"We must be frightfully early for a morning call, but I told Darcy that I simply could not wait to see my neighbours once more," Bingley chattered on in a rather agitated fashion. "You told me, did you not, Darcy, that we might do better to wait another hour?"

"I did indeed, but it does not follow that our timing was unfortunate," Darcy replied with a searching look in Elizabeth's direction. Her small smile spoke of agreement, which only confirmed in Darcy's mind that they had interrupted an altercation of some sort.

"You are, of course, most welcome, Mr Bingley. My mother and sisters are in the sitting room now, and I know they will be delighted to see you again." Elizabeth turned to face Darcy and spoke in a halting, almost hopeful tone. "I am pleased to see you as well, sir. You are welcome at Longbourn—I...um, well, that is, would you like to join us inside?"

It was clear to Darcy that she wished to say more, and the hope that began to fill his chest was sharply checked by the nervous glance she directed at Wickham as she made her invitation. Intent upon discovering the reason for his continued presence in Hertfordshire, Darcy made his excuses.

"I shall be sure to join you in but a moment. Bingley, could you escort Miss Elizabeth inside? I wish to speak to Mr Wickham."

With a smile, Bingley offered his arm and prattled away, peppering Elizabeth with questions as he returned her to the safety of her home. "Well, Miss Elizabeth, perhaps you can tell me of the rest of your travels. We were most pleased to encounter you at Pemberley this summer. In fact…"

Wickham's eyebrows rose at the mention of Elizabeth's visit to Pemberley. For not the first time, Darcy cursed Bingley's glib tongue, for he knew it would not take long for Wickham to discover his feelings for Elizabeth—that is, if he had not already done so.

"Why are you not in Newcastle?"

"What, no greetings for your old friend, Darcy?"

"We have not been friends in an age. Answer me. Why have you not taken up your commission? I made the terms of your marriage settlement perfectly clear."

"Calm yourself, old man. My wife is suffering from a sprained ankle—her own fault, mind you—and the apothecary recommended that we stay on for a time. I have written to my commanding officer explaining all. You need not always assume the worst of me."

"Experience has taught me otherwise."

Darcy observed his former companion with a shrewd eye. He did not appear to be lying this time, but that did not mean he was innocent of all mischief. There was, of course, the situation with Elizabeth that Darcy and Bingley had clearly interrupted. But how to warn him off without placing Elizabeth under further scrutiny?

"You know, I am surprised to see you here. I never

detected any preference for my wife's family on your part, even during our time in London. Yet, here you are."

"I agreed to accompany my friend who wished to return to his leased estate. Longbourn is his closest neighbour, so my presence should not be so wholly unexpected." Darcy paused before continuing, sending a hard look at his father's godson. "I will have your word that our arrangements in London will not be revealed to the family. The Bennets do not need to know of my involvement in your marriage. If my father had known of this, I cannot think but how disgusted he would be to learn his patronage was wasted on a most unworthy recipient."

Wickham bristled at the mention of Darcy's father before responding with a calculating gleam in his eye. "And what is my silence worth to you? My poor wife and I could certainly use an increase in our funds, what with the apothecary's bills to pay, you understand. Not to mention that it will be quite difficult to control Lydia's tongue, though with the promise of a few new dresses, she might be more compliant."

"It is your task to manage your wife. *I* did not run off with a child. And before you even think of extorting more money from the Darcy coffers, let me remind you that my cousin is most unhappy with the settlements I already made on your behalf. Fitzwilliam would be eager to have your commission altered to a foreign outpost, so unless you wish to join the fighting in

Spain, I suggest you rein in your speech until your departure."

Wickham's countenance paled significantly at the mention of Colonel Fitzwilliam. Scoffing inwardly, Darcy felt distinctly unimpressed with his former playmate's utter cravenness. Fitzwilliam would relish the opportunity to tan Wickham's hide—a fact the bounder must well know. In this instance, Darcy's resources extended well beyond his pecuniary advantages. Unfortunately, it did not take too long for the cur to rally, and Darcy was even more displeased by his new topic of conversation.

"I had not known that my new sister visited Pemberley this summer. Elizabeth is an enticing woman —beautiful, witty, spirited..."

"You will watch your tongue," Darcy warned in a menacing tone.

"You are far too easy to read, my old friend. Really? A country nothing? The great Fitzwilliam Darcy has finally lost his heart to a penniless bit of skirt! What would your dear, departed, lady mother say?"

Darcy reached forward and grabbed Wickham by the lapels of his coat, "I *said*, you will watch your tongue. If you disparage her again, I assure you that your remaining visit will be tortuous indeed."

Wickham wrenched himself out of Darcy's hold, angry but apparently willing to antagonise his old nemesis further.

"Poor old Darcy, to love a woman who despises you.

She preferred me, you know, and loathed the very sight of you. Even with all your wealth, I doubt Pemberley was enough to change her mind." With a smug expression, Wickham continued. "You know, I have always taken great pleasure in depriving you of what you wanted most —your father's love and now Elizabeth's. You have every advantage, yet I can best you still."

Breathing deeply to calm his temper, Darcy recognised the fallacy in Wickham's taunts. He had already lost control beyond his usual wont. He would not give the worthless lout standing before him another measure of his composure.

Pulling on the cuffs of his jacket, Darcy replied in an even, steady tone. "You have deprived me of nothing. I know who my father was—I possess no uncertainty regarding his esteem or care. As for Miss Elizabeth, my faults are my own, and your actions matter little to me." Darcy directed a scathing look at Wickham and continued. "You will, however, desist in whatever game you think you are playing with her. I saw her disquiet as we arrived, and I will not stand for it. Have you not attempted to harm her family enough?"

Before Wickham could respond, anger once again building in his eyes, Mrs Bennet ventured out from the entryway.

"There you are, Mr Wickham! Lydia has been requesting your presence for nigh on fifteen minutes! I simply cannot stand to see my poor girl suffer. Come, you must attend her at once!"

"Yes, you should see to your wife, sir," Darcy concurred before bowing in the matron's direction. "If you will excuse me, Mrs Bennet, I would like to take a short stroll in the garden before joining my friend in your parlour."

"Of course, sir." With a stiff nod that lacked the civility so frequently shown to Bingley, Mrs Bennet added, "I hope you find our gardens meet your approval, though they have lost several blooms to the season."

"I am sure they are still beautiful, ma'am," Darcy replied with what he hoped was a polite smile, though owing to the taxing nature of his recent conversation, might well have been a grimace. He quickly set off along a side path as Wickham joined his mother-in-law.

Wandering past a flowering patch of hydrangeas and pale purple asters, Darcy pondered the wisdom of returning to Hertfordshire. Though it was true that he had not intended to meet with Wickham on this trip, did he really hope to conceal all of his actions from Elizabeth regarding her sister's elopement? The current situation was untenable, yet what choice did he have? Now that he had seen her, he could not possibly leave.

"Mr Darcy?"

Startled, he turned to see Elizabeth standing before him in the garden. Sunlight brightened her chestnut locks and accentuated the healthy glow of her cheeks.

She was so very lovely, and the sight of her brought joy to Darcy's heart, even in the midst of his worry.

"Pray forgive me, Miss Elizabeth. I hope your family does not feel slighted by my delayed arrival?"

"Oh! Oh no, I merely wished to see that all is well. To be frank, my family is mostly preoccupied by Mr Bingley's return, so I do not believe they have noticed your absence. I-I thought I would invite you to join us, though I understand if you wish to remain here."

"I would be quite happy to join you. Your gardens are lovely, and I simply wished for a respite after—well, the less said the better, I suppose."

Elizabeth seemed to sense his need for a change in topic, for she reached out a hand to stroke a green-tipped hydrangea as she commented, "It is nothing to Pemberley, I dare say, but I have always enjoyed the autumn blooms we cultivate here."

"My preferences aside, Pemberley and Derbyshire need not be the standard for beauty in nature everywhere. This is quite a charming prospect."

As Darcy observed Elizabeth amongst the flowers, he realised somewhat belatedly that this was the first private conversation they had enjoyed since he left her at the inn at Lambton. She had been so often in his thoughts—the *driving* force behind most of his actions since her rejection of his hand in April—that he could hardly believe she was truly before him. Would all of their interactions be overshadowed by the mistakes of the past?

"You seem preoccupied, sir. Shall I leave you to your contemplations?"

Elizabeth regarded him intently, apprehension and worry in her eyes. Not wishing to distress her further, Darcy collected himself before presenting his arm.

"No, I thank you. I am ready to join the party."

Pleased at her acceptance of his arm, Darcy pondered the great task before him while Elizabeth led him to her family's sitting room. To remain by her side, he would have to endure the presence of the Wickhams for an as yet unknown period of time—an arduous task, indeed.

CHAPTER FIVE

✦───────✦

Any hope Elizabeth had experienced upon first encountering Mr Darcy on Longbourn's drive was checked by the tension that radiated from his person as he escorted her indoors. He had seemed so troubled when she encountered him in the garden, and though she rightly supposed that his conversation with Mr Wickham had been anything but pleasant, Elizabeth could not help but worry that she herself was contributing to his sombre demeanour. Why had he returned to Hertfordshire? Did he simply wish to support his friend? Could he possibly still care for her?

His voice, that deep, melodious rumble, brought her to a halt outside the door to her family's parlour. Eyes fixed upon her own, Mr Darcy's countenance had lost none of its reserve, though she thought perhaps a flicker of concern passed over his face.

"I-I wanted you to know that—"

"Lizzy, child! Whatever are you doing lingering about in the hall? I am sure Mr Darcy would prefer his tea and cake to standing about in such a silly manner!" Mrs Bennet's shrill tones had interrupted whatever Mr Darcy had wished to impart, and Elizabeth could only cringe in embarrassment as she led the gentleman inside.

Perhaps one day—far, far into the future—Elizabeth would reflect back upon the truly odd gathering before her with some of her habitual humour and liveliness, but sadly, that day was decidedly *not* in the offing. Lydia sat on the chaise longue, her ankle raised high under a precarious set of ruffled pillows, while her husband gathered sweets onto a plate at her loud and waspish direction. Mr Bingley hovered by the tea service, shadowing Jane as she prepared his cup as best she could, while in his anxious state the poor gentleman knocked the spoons to the floor. Mama, with her ever-fluttering lace handkerchief, was flanked by Mary and Kitty on the large sofa. Mary's face was buried in yet another book of severe sermons that she only neglected on occasion in favour of glaring at Lydia, and Kitty lounged off the opposite side in a posture that all but confirmed the absence of a governess to any interested observer. Her father, who might have derived some genuine amusement at the unfolding scene, was secluded in his book room per usual.

Unable to bear the likelihood of Mr Darcy's stony

gaze, a mortified Elizabeth gestured to the unoccupied chairs by the fireplace.

"I ought to help Jane serve the tea. Please, do sit down." With eyes still trained upon the floor, Elizabeth bustled over to Jane's side. "Mr Bingley, why do you not sit with your friend by the fire, and I shall assist Jane?" Pointing to the vacant seats, Elizabeth glanced briefly at Darcy, who sat stiff and tall with hard eyes following Mr Wickham.

"Of course, Miss Elizabeth—uh...I trust you will be a more able assistant than I—that is...I shall just go sit by Darcy, shall I?"

As Mr Bingley wandered over to his friend, Elizabeth collected the fallen spoons before Jane turned to her, a look of distress written upon her beautiful features.

"I do not know if I shall survive this visit! Mama was completely shameful while you were out of doors. I fear she will bully the poor man into a proposal, and I cannot yet tell if that is Mr Bingley's intent in returning. Perhaps he merely wishes to make amends for quitting the neighbourhood so suddenly last year." Her voice was only a murmur, but the anxiety in it was obvious.

"Mama's behaviour aside, I cannot believe that you still doubt his feelings for you," Elizabeth replied with a look of consternation.

Cannot Jane see the way Mr Bingley looks at her? As far as I can tell, he wears his heart upon his sleeve. Would that his friend do the same!

"Truly, Jane, though Mama may not know the best way to go about it, I believe she sees as clearly as the rest of us that this visit is entirely for you."

"Whatever else may happen, please promise me that you will not leave my side. I know Mama will try to arrange a private interview, and I cannot bear the scrutiny yet. Perhaps if he visits again, I may be able to maintain my composure, but not yet—not yet. I am simply too nervous!"

Though she had compassion for her sister, gentle as she was, Mr Darcy's obvious tension in company with the Wickhams and Elizabeth's own current unease with Mr Wickham in particular, rendered Jane's plight rather trifling by comparison.

And then there was the matter of Mr Darcy himself. Why had he returned? *He cannot possibly still love me, no—but, what if he does?* Hope was a fickle thing indeed.

"Why do you not take Mr Bingley his tea and join the gentlemen by the fire? I shall be swift to join you, I promise, and then you can converse among friends. That cannot be so intimidating, surely?"

"You will not be long?" Jane queried, her disquiet obviously lessened by Elizabeth's reassurances.

"Of course not. I simply mean to prepare Mr Darcy's tea."

At her sister's nod, Elizabeth turned back to the parlour table, searching for the lemon slices. As she added a slice to a freshly poured cup, she inwardly marvelled at her knowledge of Mr Darcy's preferences. Perhaps she had always paid a bit more attention to the gentleman than she had previously cared to admit.

"I see you have anticipated me, Sister."

An unwelcome voice at her shoulder halted Elizabeth's progress, her spine stiffening as she realised the close proximity of Mr Wickham.

"Let me see...no sugar, lemon wedge. For shame, Elizabeth! You must know by now that I take my tea with milk and sugar. After all, one must enjoy the sweet things in life." Mr Wickham sent her a leering grin that set Elizabeth's teeth on edge. "Now why is this particular drink so familiar?" Wickham pondered, tapping his chin in thought that was clearly feigned.

"Oh, I do not know," Elizabeth countered, her voice airy and everything insincere. "Perhaps you are not so familiar with the customs of polite society as I once thought."

With a tight smile and no opportunity for a rejoinder, Elizabeth left to join her sister and the Netherfield gentlemen.

"Your tea, sir."

"Thank you, Miss Elizabeth." Mr Darcy took his cup, and though she could not be certain, Elizabeth thought she observed a small smile cross his visage as he peered down into the porcelain. His sombre mien returned swiftly, though his eyes conveyed sincere concern as they flickered between her and Mr Wickham. "You are well, I trust?"

"Of course. I believe I have told you before that my courage always rises at every attempt to intimidate me," Elizabeth assured him, her tone light and teasing.

Rather than allaying his unease, her attempt at levity only brought about an even sterner expression on the gentleman's face as he directed a cold, piercing gaze at her brother-in-law.

Sensing the perturbation of his friend, Mr Bingley gallantly addressed the newly married couple. "I say, I have been quite remiss in offering my congratulations on your nuptials."

Preening at the attention, Lydia replied, "Thank you, Mr Bingley. My dear Wickham and I are so exceedingly happy! We were married in London, you know, which is far more fashionable than stuffy old Meryton. But then, you must know all about it already for Mr Da—"

"Lydia my sweet," Mr Wickham interrupted, glancing nervously at Darcy before continuing. "You must not bore the gentlemen with talk of the wedding. After all, lace and fripperies matter little to anyone other than the bride."

After a brittle smile and a sharp look at his wife, Wickham turned to Mr Bingley. "As my wife said, we are truly quite joyful at our union, and I certainly cannot repine the connexions I have obtained. My sisters are everything delightful, are they not?"

Staring down into her teacup, Elizabeth could feel Wickham's gaze settle quite pointedly in her direction.

"Have you any news of the Gardiners, Miss Elizabeth? That is—I hope they are well. I greatly enjoyed making their acquaintance this summer," Mr Darcy interjected.

Stunned into silence, Elizabeth could only stare at Mr Darcy as she tried to think of something to say that would not disclose the information she had recently received from her aunt. If only his otherwise gracious attempt at redirecting the conversation could have been about anything else!

"You are acquainted with my brother and his wife?" Mrs Bennet's surprised voice rang out across the parlour.

"Yes, madam. I had the pleasure of meeting them in Derbyshire at my estate while they were travelling with Miss Elizabeth."

"Lizzy, you never mentioned meeting Mr Darcy on your travels!"

Wincing at her mother's scolding tone, Elizabeth chanced a look at Mr Darcy only to see him studiously observing his boots. How had this day become such a muddle?

"'Twas no secret, Mama. There simply was not the opportunity to tell you, what with all the events that transpired upon my return." Elizabeth could not help glancing briefly at Lydia and her husband before quickly returning her focus to her tea.

Looking between Elizabeth and Mr Darcy, Lydia suddenly exclaimed, "Oh, so that is how he—"

"Lydia, my love. I believe you require some fresh air —a turn in the garden perhaps? Come, let me assist you." Without so much as another word, Mr Wickham swept his wife into his arms and carried her out of the room, her wrapped ankle leading the way out the parlour door.

"What a dashing young man! That is, I am sure he meant to properly take his leave of you gentlemen," Mrs Bennet surmised, looking out the door in confusion after the Wickhams' hasty exit.

"It is no matter, madam, though I believe Bingley and I ought to depart. We have business with his steward." Mr Darcy looked directly at his friend who was still staring longingly at Jane. "Bingley?"

"What? Oh yes, quite right." Collecting himself, Mr Bingley stood before addressing Jane. "I do hope we may call again tomorrow?"

With a slight blush in her cheeks, Jane quietly replied, "We shall always be happy to welcome you, sir."

Together with her sister and at their mother's insistence, Elizabeth saw the gentlemen to the door. After they donned their coats and hats and mounted their steeds, Elizabeth watched them ride off, overcome with wretchedness that Mr Darcy had to endure what was perhaps one of the worst and most awkward calls that had ever taken place at Longbourn—a feat of some significance. If only she had the power to wish the irksome Wickhams far, far away, and the ability to wish the handsome, serious gentleman from Derbyshire back.

CHAPTER SIX

❖——————————❖

A thick, heavy blanket of mist shrouded the gentle rolling hills of the Hertfordshire landscape from Darcy's eyes. Autumnal leaves, in all their shifting hues, peeked through the veil at the edge of the woods that stood near the boundary between Longbourn and Netherfield. It seemed even when the path before him remained unclear, Darcy would always be drawn unfailingly back to *her*.

His restless mount shifted beneath him, agitated by the rigidity in his master's bearing. Awakened repeatedly from his slumber, plagued as he was by visions of a troubled Elizabeth, an early morning ride had seemed to be a welcome reprieve. The haziness of his surroundings, however, only perturbed his already muddled thoughts.

How could he possibly remain in company with the Wickhams without his secrets from the past summer coming to light? Yet, how could he possibly leave Elizabeth to endure their company alone? The mere thought of abandoning her to fend off Wickham unaided caused Darcy to feel ill. He could scarcely withstand returning to Netherfield without her while the scoundrel remained at Longbourn.

What would Elizabeth think if she knew I was the cause of her present suffering? Surely, I could have tried harder to separate Miss Lydia from her unscrupulous beau? The thousands of pounds spent upon the marriage might have induced a more palatable bridegroom to accept a ruined, thoughtless girl like Lydia Bennet.

Then again, Darcy recalled the new Mrs Wickham's stubborn refusal to leave the squalor of the seedy London apartments where he had found them before the marriage. It did not matter how many times he turned over the possibilities in his mind, Darcy always came to the inevitable conclusion: preserving Elizabeth's respectability was worth everything, even the irksome prospect of gaining George Wickham as a brother. There was nothing for it. He must remain in Hertfordshire while Bingley continued his courting of Miss Bennet, and while he did not intend to woo Elizabeth until after the Wickhams' departure, he could still be the support she needed during what had to be an exceedingly unsettling time.

Lost in his thoughts, he had allowed his stallion his head, and unlike Darcy, his mount had little trouble in finding the path back to Netherfield. After handing the reins to an eager young stable boy, Darcy climbed the brick steps of the manor home's front entrance and passed his greatcoat and hat to Mr Jennings, whose tense bearing belied his calm, usually unruffled appearance. Shrieks emanated from the front sitting room, and as Darcy followed the distressed sounds, the butler called out to him.

"Sir, I-I thought it best to inform you the mistress has lately returned to Netherfield."

"Mistress?" Darcy replied, confusion furrowing his brows until a particularly loud screech reached his ears. "Do you mean to say that Miss Bingley has arrived, Jennings?"

"Yes, sir. Only just."

At times like these, Darcy truly hated being right. Why had Bingley left his sister a *note*?

"Have you completely lost your senses, Charles?" Miss Bingley's brutal chastisement of her brother had finally reached a volume that could not be contained by the sitting room door.

"Do you know what you have done? You have forced me to return to this savage little wilderness to rescue you from the clutches of that fortune-hunting family! And to make matters worse, you have brought Mr Darcy back within reach of that scheming Miss Eliza! You saw how she threw herself at him at Pemberley! How could you do such a thing!"

Bristling with indignation, Darcy swiftly entered the room. Bingley sat with his arms crossed, glaring at his sister, while Miss Bingley was so startled by his sudden appearance that she fell silent. After taking a moment to collect herself, she rallied with a pitiful attempt to gain Darcy's support.

"Surely, you must agree that Netherfield, charming though it is, cannot provide my brother with the most pleasing society? I had thought he intended to give up the lease altogether and search for an estate in the north —closer to Derbyshire perhaps?"

Her honeyed tones set Darcy's teeth on edge just as easily as her unladylike shrieks. There was something he found distinctly unappealing about dishonesty.

"I am afraid I cannot agree with you. The company in Hertfordshire has not been lacking. I believe Bingley and I shall be well entertained during our stay," Darcy replied with as much nonchalance as he could muster.

Turning her attention to her brother, Miss Bingley asked, "And how *long* shall this stay be?"

"Well, Caroline, if you had actually let me finish earlier, I would have told you my intent is to stay until Miss Jane Bennet has accepted my hand or turned me away. I am sorry you are so displeased at the possibility of gaining such an agreeable sister, but I shall not be moved. I love Miss Bennet, and that is all you need know of the matter."

Darcy had to admit he was rather impressed with his

friend. Bingley did not back down, despite his sister's vitriol, and judging by her expression, his friend's firm stance was unanticipated. What troubled Darcy, however, was the calculating gleam in Miss Bingley's eyes as she took in her brother's resolve.

"Very well, Charles. If you are so determined, then I suppose I must change my gown and remove the dust from the road ere we depart." And without so much as another word, Miss Bingley turned to exit the room.

She had almost passed through the door before Bingley had recovered his wits enough to ask, "Depart?"

"Why yes! I assume you mean to call on Miss Bennet this morning?" After a weak nod from her brother, Miss Bingley continued. "Then I must accompany you! Indeed, how would it look to poor Miss Bennet if she knew I was in the county and failed to call?" With a smile filled with false sweetness, Miss Bingley quit the room.

"What just happened, Darcy?"

"I cannot say I know for sure, but I doubt your sister has changed her mind regarding the Bennets in a matter of minutes. My conjecture is she means to interfere, which you must agree, she cannot do while sitting alone at Netherfield."

"Blast!" Bingley slapped his hands on the armrests of his chair, frustration written plain upon his face. "I am anxious enough as it is. I do not need Caroline complicating matters with Miss Bennet!"

"Can you not simply return her to the Hursts?" Darcy asked, his tone laced with sympathy.

"With her current attitude, Hurst would send her straight back. She is, after all, my responsibility until she marries. No, if I mean to do this properly, I must learn to manage her—for Miss Bennet's sake."

While Darcy applauded his friend's efforts, after a single carriage ride of three miles he was tempted to ask if the Bingleys had any other relations with whom Miss Bingley could reside—preferably living in the Scottish Highlands or perhaps the Isle of Man. Shaking off the negative diatribe concerning Meryton and its surrounds, Darcy entered Longbourn eager despite all circumstances to see Elizabeth.

The two eldest Bennet daughters were no doubt surprised to see Miss Bingley, and Elizabeth in particular looked upon that lady's attention to her elder sister with understandable suspicion.

"My dear Miss Bennet! It has been so long since we were last together. Come, you must tell all that has occurred in my absence."

"Actually, Caroline, Miss Bennet and I were hoping to take a walk in the garden, were we not?"

"Oh nonsense! You must leave the ladies to become reacquainted. I am sure there will be time for walks aplenty, though I do hope the weather does not grow too cold. We would not wish dear Miss Bennet to catch a chill, especially as she seems so susceptible to trifling colds!"

Elizabeth's poor sister sat awkwardly between the feuding pair, and while Bingley appeared agitated, Elizabeth looked as though she would skewer Miss Bingley if given the chance. Just as Darcy was about to speak to her, he was anticipated by Wickham.

"My dear, you seem distressed. Are you sure you do not wish for a stroll in the garden? There was a matter I wished to speak of, if you recall."

"Again, I have no notion of why that would be necessary. There cannot be two people in the room with less to speak of than the pair of us," Elizabeth replied evenly, looking past Wickham's shoulder to the window beyond.

"I find I would not mind the opportunity to stretch my legs. Perhaps I could accompany you, Miss Elizabeth." Darcy offered.

Just as Elizabeth looked up, her eyes finding his as a hopeful smile spread across her lovely visage, Mrs Wickham intervened.

"Whyever would you wish to leave if you have just arrived? Besides, Lizzy does not need so many gallant escorts," Mrs Wickham opined, sending a glare at her new husband. "If gentlemen truly found her so interesting, she would yet be married, but then again, I suppose I cannot blame her for rejecting Mr Collins."

"Lydia!" Mortification bloomed across Elizabeth's

face, and before Darcy could think of a change in topic, Mrs Bennet joined her youngest daughter.

"I certainly can blame her. To think I must one day make way for Charlotte Lucas when Lizzy could have been the next mistress of Longbourn! And with her wild ways, who knows if she will ever receive another offer!"

"Pray excuse me. I must—I must speak to Mary in the music room." Without another word, Elizabeth swiftly rose and left the parlour. As early as Darcy could manage, he made his excuses and departed in search of her, his mind reeling at the treatment of his beloved by her own family. He had only just left the room when he found her pacing in the hall and called out her name.

At his voice, she stopped pacing, her head drooping down as she uttered in a soft tone, "I apologise for my mother and sister. While I know you are well aware of their lack of decorum, it pains me to have you witness such an appalling display."

"I beg of you, do not discomfit yourself any further on my behalf. I simply wished to see you were well." The weariness in her fine eyes tore at Darcy's heart, and wishing to restore her vibrancy, he continued. "Though I suppose I ought to share in any mortification you currently bear. After all, it is not every day one finds oneself in the esteemed company of Mr Collins—yet, *I* was the last man you could ever..."

A brief flicker of panic crossed Elizabeth's face before she noted the small upward turn of Darcy's lips. Letting out a short bark of laughter, Elizabeth responded with a twinkle in her eye. "If it comforts you, by then Mr Collins was already married." Her smile of humour faded quickly as she said, "You cannot know how long I have wished to apologise for that day. You did not deserve the cruel words I uttered without thought."

"Pray do not concern—"

"Lizzy, whatever are you doing in the hall, dear child?" Mr Bennet had poked his head out of his book room and was now walking towards them.

"I needed a brief change of scenery, Papa. That is all."

Mr Bennet looked askance at his second eldest, then fixed his attention on Darcy. "I imagine all the discussions of lace and parties has quite taxed your forbearance, sir. Perhaps you would prefer a game of chess in my study?"

Not wishing to leave Elizabeth, Darcy began to demur. "That is very kind, Mr Bennet, though I would not wish to be rude and abandon the ladies or my friend, for that matter."

"Nonsense, nonsense! I am sure Mr Bingley is suitably occupied, and as for the ladies, Lizzy has often been my only challenger at the game and is welcome to join us. What say you, Lizzy? Care to trounce your old Papa?" he asked with a twinkle in the eyes that so resembled Elizabeth's.

"If Mr Darcy has no objections, I would be pleased to join you." Tilting her head in his direction, Darcy's pulse quickened as her smile turned mischievous. "Well, sir, can you brook losing to a lady?" she challenged, her humour restored.

"You seem quite confident, Miss Elizabeth," Darcy quipped with a smile. "I look forward to a stimulating match."

Once Mr Bennet had led them into his study, he encouraged them to play the opening game, declaring he would happily challenge the winner. After settling himself behind his desk, the Bennet patriarch picked up a weathered copy of Herodotus and left Darcy and Elizabeth to themselves; however, Darcy suspected the older gentleman was not so wholly absorbed in his reading as he pretended.

Trying to settle his nerves and act as though Elizabeth's father was not keenly observing their interactions, Darcy focused on the game before him. It only took a few moves for him to realise that Elizabeth was quite skilled.

"You play very well, Miss Elizabeth."

"Thank you, sir. Papa began teaching me when I was seven or eight. He captained the chess team at Oxford when he attended, so I have benefited from a very capable teacher. Mama, however, does not approve, as she does not believe any gentleman would wish for a wife who could rival him in skill."

"Well, in this instance, your mother is wrong."

As he lifted his gaze to her face, a becoming blush spread across her cheeks.

"I have always been intrigued by the nature of chess —the seemingly endless paths to victory, even its unpredictability at times," Elizabeth mused, as she pondered her next move.

"'Tis not always so unpredictable, for if you are familiar with your opponent, you tend to pick up on their strategies and oft used gambits. Such knowledge allows you to plan your moves accordingly."

"And if one miscalculates? What then?" Elizabeth asked, with a look in her eyes that Darcy could not interpret. "In my experience, the game can be easily lost when you fail to truly understand your opponent. Opportunities can be missed, and correcting your course is sometimes impossible."

Darcy could not be certain they were still speaking of chess, and the import of Elizabeth's words troubled him. Just as he began to respond, a cry from Mrs Bennet was heard in the hall concerning Elizabeth's whereabouts.

"Well, my Lizzy, it seems your mother has need of you—although it appears you have routed Mr Darcy quite effectively!"

Darcy looked down at the board, and indeed Mr Bennet was correct. In only a few moves, Elizabeth would claim victory.

"Thank you, and you are right, I suppose I ought to return to Mama."

As she began to rise, Darcy thought back to her cryptic statements on missed opportunities, and before he could stop himself, he quickly interjected in a soft tone, "I do not believe that correcting one's course is ever impossible. It only takes the ability to see a different path beyond the one intended. As long as the desired goal is fixed and unchangeable, sometimes it is simply a sheer act of will."

Looking deeply into his eyes, Elizabeth whispered, "An ever-fixed mark."

Darcy's heart was in his throat as she turned and left the room.

CHAPTER SEVEN

"I cannot understand her. Lizzy?" Elizabeth startled at Jane's gentle prod of her hand.

"I am sorry, Jane. You have caught me wool-gathering. Of what were you speaking?"

With a huff, her sister rolled onto her side and answered, "Miss Bingley, of course! Why do you think she has returned? She made it quite clear in London that our acquaintance was at an end."

The two eldest Bennet sisters were huddled together on Elizabeth's bed—a regular occurrence after the family retired for the night. Ordinarily, Elizabeth would have been thoroughly engaged with the topic at hand, particularly as it concerned her sister's rekindled courtship. However, her thoughts continuously strayed to her afternoon's chess match.

"I believe you know very well what my opinion will be when it concerns Miss Bingley."

"She cannot be all bad, you know."

"Ah, my dear sweet Jane, I am sorry to inform you that whatever goodness that lady possesses remains a mystery to me. I thought it clear that her purpose was to distract you from speaking to her brother. Poor Mr Bingley looked quite put out when I returned to the drawing room. Were you able to converse with him at all?"

"I confess I was not. Why were you with Papa for so long, if you do not mind me asking?"

Elizabeth continued her observation of the canopy. With his sudden return to Hertfordshire, she had not intended to share her thoughts on Mr Darcy with Jane, as keeping her disappointed hopes private seemed the best course. After their discussion over chess, however, perhaps she might gain clarity if she dared to voice her desires aloud.

"Mr Darcy and I were playing chess. Papa invited us to join him after we were discovered in the hall."

"You were with Mr Darcy? I hope that was not too unsettling for you."

Jane was all that was sympathetic, but once again, Elizabeth felt that mayhap it was time to enlighten her dearest sister of her complete change of heart regarding the gentleman. Anything else felt remarkably deceptive.

"'Twas not unsettling at all. In fact, I have come to

enjoy his company. I know we have not spoken much of my stay in Derbyshire. The news of Lydia's elopement all but rendered my new feelings irrelevant, but I confess that I have come to esteem Mr Darcy greatly. He is the best man of my acquaintance."

The shock written upon Jane's face was nearly comical before it softened into a look of understanding. "Oh my dear, dear Lizzy! Do you love him?"

"I confess I do," Elizabeth softly admitted. "I had thought the situation to be hopeless, for how could he possibly entertain the notion of tying himself to our family when it now includes Mr Wickham? I did not think he could love me so well as that, but...but today in Papa's study, I think he was trying to tell me that he loves me still. Of course, we could not speak plainly, but even so..."

Clasping her hand, Jane softly uttered, "Of course, he still loves you, for how could he not?"

Wiping away the tears that had suddenly clouded her vision, Elizabeth tightened her hold on Jane's hand. "Thank you, Jane." With her heart a bit lighter, Elizabeth was able to find sleep.

The next morning Elizabeth awoke to find her sister still sleeping beside her. While the previous night's confessions had provided a much-needed release, she was suddenly filled with a restless energy that could only be satisfied by a cool, morning ramble.

Dressing quietly so as not to awaken Jane, Elizabeth

twisted her hair into a simple chignon and grabbed a bonnet as she silently exited her bedroom. Stopping briefly at the kitchens, Elizabeth thanked Cook for a small parcel of fresh, hot rolls before making her way to the front vestibule to don her half boots.

Crisp, clean, autumn air filled Elizabeth's lungs as she set off on her regular path through the back gardens and out of the gate into the pastureland beyond. Just as she closed the gate, an unwelcome voice startled her.

"I see I have finally caught you alone, Sister, though I did not expect you quite so early. Country hours, indeed."

In that moment, Elizabeth struggled to recall why she had ever found Mr Wickham's voice and manners appealing. Now, the slightest whisper of his hollow charm was utterly maddening.

"Were you waiting for me, sir? Though I have no experience in such matters, I find it highly irregular that a recently wed gentleman would seek the company of his new sister-in-law to the point of anticipating her on her morning's stroll."

"As I have said before, we have issues to discuss."

"And *I* say we do not. Good day, sir," Elizabeth pronounced with such feeling that Mr Wickham could be in no doubt of her desire for his departure.

"He will never marry you, you know," Wickham called out to Elizabeth after she turned to walk away.

Shocked by his audacity, Elizabeth turned once

more to face the most vile man of her acquaintance. Once he saw that her attention was engaged, he continued.

"I see your fondness for him, but Darcy's family would never allow him to wed an insignificant country girl such as yourself. He is meant for a far more splendid match or so I heard repeatedly in our youth. Not that Darcy himself would ever condescend to make an offer in the first place, despite your...charms." Wickham's gaze roamed over her form, granting Elizabeth the fleeting urge to cast up her accounts.

"What business is this of yours, Mr Wickham? I will ask you plainly, please leave me be."

Ignoring her request, he continued with a wounded expression. "You cannot know how put out your defection has made me. I thought us friends, yet you would champion the very man who, out of nothing more than jealousy, has denied me my rightful inheritance."

Astonished at his temerity, Elizabeth decided then and there that simply ignoring Mr Wickham was no longer an option.

"As we are now brother and sister, I hope you will not take offence if I speak openly with you, sir."

Mr Wickham merely smiled smugly. "Of course. Pray speak on."

"You say Mr Darcy is jealous of you, but for my part, I cannot imagine why. For truly, if anyone has cause to be jealous, it would most certainly be you."

Wickham's smile tightened. "Come now. You cannot be serious."

"I have thought on the fraudulent tales you have told me many times over the past several months, and yes, I am fully aware of the compensation you received for the living. In all honesty, I must say that I now struggle to understand how I ever gave your assertions *any* credit." Elizabeth kept her voice calm and level. "Even if what you say has merit, and the late Mr Darcy did favour you so strongly, why should that inspire such a degree of jealousy in the present Mr Darcy who, by all other accounts I have heard, is an honourable man? You, however, possess none of Mr Darcy's wealth, and I am sure that many, yourself included, covet his connexions, his estate, and his position in society. And to all this, your deficiencies appear only greater when one considers his character."

"H-his character!" Wickham spluttered.

"Yes, indeed! I speak of his qualities that will always prove elusive to a man such as you—his upright nature, his innate goodness, his intelligence, and his determination to do what is best for those he loves. I am sure the late Mr Darcy must have found you amusing, a diversion of sorts from the pressures he bore in his position, but after hearing the reports of his character during my travels in Derbyshire, it is abundantly clear which young man would have garnered his approbation and no doubt his love."

Mr Wickham's countenance was frightening as he declared in a menacing tone, "Do not speak of matters you cannot possibly comprehend!"

Trembling, Elizabeth stood her ground. "Oh, I comprehend more than you would like! How dare you speak to me of friendship! You must think me a simpleton if you believe I would welcome a renewal of our earlier acquaintance. How could I feel any loyalty to the scoundrel who almost brought ruin down on my entire family! Believe me, I know exactly whose honour saved my family's reputation, and it was not yours. I am only relieved that you failed to cause similar devastation to Mr Darcy's poor, sweet sister."

Angry tears flowed down Elizabeth's face as Mr Wickham stared at her in shock. That she would have knowledge of his attempt to ruin Georgiana Darcy and abscond with her dowry had clearly never occurred to him.

Having decided that she had said enough, Elizabeth made to turn and leave, but as she did so, she spied her two youngest sisters watching them out the windows overlooking the garden. Kitty stood, supporting her sister's weight, while Lydia stared at the pair of them with a murderous expression. Unwilling to deal with her sister's misplaced jealousy over the miscreant she had married, Elizabeth attempted to calm herself as she dismissed the man in front of her.

"I believe we understand one another now, Mr Wickham. Pray excuse me. I would like to still partake of my morning's exercise, and perhaps you ought to see to the needs of your wife."

Not even bothering to confirm the blackguard's return to the house, Elizabeth nearly ran to the shelter of the orchard. Upon reaching her destination, she collapsed against a tree, utterly spent from the unexpected confrontation. Taking a seat amongst the fallen leaves, Elizabeth wiped the tears from her face, unsure as to why she was crying. While frightened at times during their encounter, above all, she felt an abundance of relief that she had finally expressed her true opinion of that vile, hateful man!

Considering the Wickhams' extended residence in Longbourn, her speech was perhaps imprudent, but try as she might, Elizabeth could not bring herself to regret it. After regaining a semblance of equanimity, she rose and dusted the broken leaves from her morning gown and made her way back towards the house. Hoping to enter unseen, her attempt was dashed by the sound of carriage wheels upon Longbourn's drive. The Netherfield party had arrived, and just as Mr Darcy stepped down from the carriage, his concerned gaze informing Elizabeth of her failure to hide her earlier distress, an angry wail was heard from the interior of the house.

CHAPTER EIGHT

"I thought I told you to stay away from her!!"

"I do not take orders from *you*, woman."

The Wickhams' angry words were heard by all who stood outside Longbourn's door. Mr Darcy's eyes rested solely upon Elizabeth, who he could very well see was flooded with embarrassment by all that was taking place within. Concerned by this display of marital strife occurring within her own home, Darcy could only feel that somehow he was the cause of it all.

"Um, well, perhaps we ought not to intrude upon your family today, Miss Elizabeth," Mr Bingley ventured, his demeanour hesitant.

"But I promised sweet Miss Bennet I would visit today, Charles! What would she think if she knew we had arrived and then departed so quickly!" Miss Bingley scolded, though Darcy could see she looked positively giddy at the evidence of such vulgarity. "After all, the Bennets are all that is genteel, are they not?" she asked her brother before continuing with a pointed look. "They could never truly give us, their dear friends, any cause for embarrassment. I am sure Miss Eliza would agree that there is no cause to fear any lack of decorum in her home. Is that not right?"

Before Elizabeth could even respond to such a speech, Miss Bingley had taken her brother's arm and steered him towards the parlour. Left alone with Elizabeth, Darcy stopped her before she could follow the others.

"Miss Elizabeth, I am—"

"I do not think there is much that can be said after all you have witnessed."

Her humiliation over the morning's events was plain to see, as was her inclination to retreat into the house. Though he desired to stay in her presence unattended, he did not want to disconcert her unduly. "I only wished to see you are well. You seemed distressed before the altercation occurred, and I-I wanted to offer my assistance, should you require it."

A small flickering of hope seemed to kindle in her expressive eyes before they shuttered. "Indeed, I am well. Truly—I merely expressed my displeasure towards my new brother this morning and my disclosures seem to have vexed him somewhat." His frown must have caught her notice, for she sought to alleviate his concern with a mischievous grin. "Perhaps I am partly to blame for what occurred just now, but I cannot feel any true remorse. Disguise, would you not agree, is abhorrent?"

Darcy's lips twitched, a slight smile creeping across his visage. "Just so, madam." Offering his arm, the pair crossed under the front portico to brave what lay beyond.

All in all, the scene in Longbourn's parlour was better than Darcy had expected, though it was clear tensions remained high. The fact that order had been restored amongst the various inhabitants was clearly owed to the presence of Mr Bennet, who sat in a stiff, high-backed chair, glaring quite pointedly at his son-in-law. Darcy was slightly surprised the patriarch had troubled himself to intervene, yet he supposed even the most indolent father would take umbrage at any man who dared to speak to one of his daughters in the fashion Wickham had done only moments before.

That the argument had caused a degree of alarm in most of the family present could not be doubted. Miss Bennet's usually serene calm had deserted her, leaving her surprisingly more loquacious than Darcy had ever before seen. She chattered away in a rather timorous fashion to both of the guests, and Miss Bingley for once could do naught but let her speak, as astonished as anyone by the behaviour of the eldest Bennet daughter. Miss Mary and Miss Catherine were both glancing back and forth between the Wickhams, one in disapproving vexation and the other in confusion. Mrs Bennet, too, it seemed could not understand what had just transpired, though her preoccupation was focused solely on her son-in-law. The gentleman in question sat as far from his wife as was possible in the somewhat crowded drawing room, staring pointedly out the window and ignoring the occupants within. Mrs Wickham sat sullenly on the sofa next to her mother, though Darcy could not like the gleam of anger in her eyes as she watched Elizabeth enter the room.

"Ah, Lizzy, so good of you to join us! And you as well, Mr Darcy." Mr Bennet nodded his head in greeting, to which Darcy gave a polite bow.

Recalled to her duties as hostess, Mrs Bennet echoed her husband's greeting. "Why yes, it is indeed a pleasure to welcome our neighbours from Netherfield again." Turning to Mr Bingley she continued. "You know, I have not forgotten that you had promised to dine with us before your departure last year. We would be more than delighted to have both you and your sister for dinner later this week—in fact, you can name the day!" Mrs Bennet gave a cautious glance in Darcy's direction. "Your friend is, of course, welcome to join us as well. I promise we set a fine table."

"That is very kind, madam. I should be happy to dine with your family."

At his response, Mrs Wickham huffed inelegantly, and for once, even Mrs Bennet chastised her. "Mind your manners—and stop slouching! It is most unbecoming of a married woman to slouch."

"Yes, Mama," Lydia conceded, though if her posture changed a whit, Darcy could not tell. "I did not mean to offend anyone. I suppose I am simply surprised to see Mr Darcy so much of late," she drawled dully while she conducted a thorough inspection of her fingernails.

This utterance seemed to catch the attention of her husband, for Wickham's gaze turned rapidly from the front lawn to his wife, his eyes filled with a gravity that was rare.

"Our guests have displayed a great fondness for the present company," Mr Bennet quipped, with a displeased look at his youngest. "They pay us a noble compliment in abandoning their country pursuits for our front parlour—for what is hunting to tea, cakes, and fine conversation, eh?"

Not often flummoxed in company, for Darcy chiefly preferred observation to interacting with his fellow men, he could, however, quite readily admit that Elizabeth's father was far too enigmatic for his liking. While he seemed to have detected a preference on Darcy's part for his second eldest, Darcy could not determine if he looked upon such a possibility with approval or disdain. Was he speaking in earnest, or employing the subtle mockery that Darcy had witnessed on more than one occasion?

Bingley answered, his levity restored. "I can assure

you that we are quite pleased to receive such affability! I can only shoot birds for so long. Undoubtedly, the company I find here is far preferable."

As he turned to look upon Miss Bennet, Mrs Wickham rolled her eyes in a pronounced fashion as she said, "That is all well and good, I suppose, but what I meant to say earlier was that I am surprised to see Mr Darcy so soon after my wedding in London."

An uneasy pause filled the room before Miss Catherine declared with sudden recognition, "You *did* mention that Mr Darcy attended your wedding! I thought you must have been joking!"

Mr Wickham's face looked thunderous as he glared at his wife, while Mrs Bennet looked between Lydia and Darcy and stuttered, "But I-I thought you and Mr Wickham...that is...but—why were *you* at my daughter's wedding?"

At that moment, Darcy wished the parlour floor would swallow him whole. He did not know where to look, though a brief glance at his friend confirmed Bingley's wholehearted astonishment. Miss Bingley, however, looked both shocked and highly perturbed—her gaze shifting to Elizabeth in distaste.

Taking advantage of Darcy's silence, Mrs Wickham continued in a blithe tone. "Oh, did you not know, Mama?"

"That is enough, Lydia!" Wickham hissed, anger clearly written upon his face.

Unbothered by her husband's protests, Mrs Wickham proceeded to disclose that which Darcy had never meant to come to light. "Mr Darcy is the one who found us at the inn in London. I saw him often at Gracechurch Street in the days before my wedding, although I confess I know not what he was doing in Uncle Gardiner's study at all hours of the day and night."

Satisfied by the staggering silence that met her divulgence, Mrs Wickham sat back and eyed her husband with rebellious pleasure. The reactions to her story varied greatly across the room. Miss Bingley observed the Wickhams with open disgust, Bingley's shock had only increased, and the rest of the Bennets looked upon Darcy with astonishment.

Darcy could scarcely take it all in, so consumed was he by the *only* person's response who truly mattered. As he turned his head briefly to regard Elizabeth, he could see her eyes were closed, though the mortification upon her countenance was there all the same.

Ashen-faced, Mr Bennet queried, "It was not my brother Gardiner who paid this man's debts and brought about the marriage, was it? It—it was you?"

Darcy could do no more than give a brief, very stiff nod.

"But why? Why, sir? Why would you do this extraordinary thing? Our family can be nothing to you."

Though he tried, Darcy could not help but look at Elizabeth, only to find that she too was watching him expectantly, her brilliant eyes locking on his. Struggle as he might, his endeavour to hide his emotions from her failed, comprehension dawning as she gasped, her hand lifting to cover her mouth. Her eyes began to well with tears. Darcy could not look away from her obvious anguish.

What possible explanation could he give? Perhaps explaining his guilt over the misdeeds of his father's godson, compounded by his lack of warning when the reprobate first entered Meryton would be enough to satisfy Mr Bennet's request, but the half-truth stuck in Darcy's mouth before he could even utter it. Though a satisfactory reason on its own, Darcy knew that ever since encountering a distraught Elizabeth at the inn at Lambton, any action he had taken regarding the Wickhams had been solely and unreservedly for her. To tell anything less, would be a falsehood, and he could not bring himself to mar their acquaintance any further by denying his continued love for her.

When Mr Bennet looked as though he would press for a response, Darcy rose from his chair. "Pray excuse me, I fear I cannot give you the answers you seek. I beg your pardon, but I must leave. Good day to you all."

Barely recalling what he said to the butler as he took his greatcoat and hat, Darcy fled the house and made his way towards the stable. The young groom, having been caught by surprise, scrambled to ready one of the carriage horses for Darcy as the gentleman began forming rapid plans for his departure from the area.

For how could he stay? The despair in Elizabeth's eyes as the truth was revealed was simply too painful for Darcy to endure.

He mounted Bingley's horse, promising the groom to return the beast with one of Bingley's men after his arrival at Netherfield, and turned towards the main drive, girding himself for a hard ride to calm his roiling thoughts. But before he could dash out of Longbourn's main gate, a slight figure ran out of the house and placed herself boldly in his path.

CHAPTER NINE

⸻✦⸻

S itting in stunned silence in her family's drawing room, Elizabeth's hand still rested over her mouth as Mr Darcy bid his hasty adieu. Despite the general bewilderment of the room, she could think on nothing except the one fact she had not allowed herself to truly believe until that moment: that Mr Darcy had done everything for her—only her—and all because he loved her still. He had braved every embarrassment, every degradation that scouring the seedy inns of London could afford, to unite two utterly selfish individuals and save her family from scorn and ridicule, and it had all been for her and her alone.

The look in his eyes—such deep affection and yearning—how did I fail to notice it before? I have been a blind fool!

Could she ever come to deserve a love so ardent and sincere? Elizabeth supposed the answer did not truly matter, as Mr Darcy seemed to offer such devotion willingly, despite her many faults and offences against him.

As the occupants of the parlour slowly roused themselves from their amazed quietude, she noticed Jane's smile directed solely upon her. Elizabeth nodded her head in acknowledgement, while poor Mr Bingley received the brunt of her mother's perplexed musings.

"But surely, you must have known something of your friend's assistance! I still cannot understand what has happened. Why would Mr Darcy have met with my brother over Lydia's marriage? 'Tis most unsettling!"

"Madam, I assure you I know absolutely nothing of the matter! Quite frankly, I am just as bewildered as anyone!"

As her mother began to complain of her nerves, Elizabeth caught her father's questioning gaze, and before he could speak what was so clearly on his mind, she excused herself from the room to pursue Mr Darcy. There had been too many misunderstandings, too many dashed hopes, to allow any sort of confusion to remain between them. She must tell him—nay, she needed to let him know how much she truly and unreservedly loved him.

Espying him by the stables, mounting a carriage horse and preparing to leave, Elizabeth ran out to the main drive and placed herself firmly in his path. This conversation was absolutely necessary, in fact, if she had only been brave enough to raise the topic after reading her aunt's letter, she might have spared him the humiliation he had just experienced.

As he approached, she called out, "Please, do not go. I would speak to you, if I may."

Though she could sense her request ran contrary to his wishes, he nevertheless dismounted and approached her.

"I do not know why you would wish for my presence. Not when it is I and I alone who is responsible for what you have endured with that cur residing in your home." Mr Darcy took off his hat and ran a hand through his hair, rendering him slightly dishevelled and more discomposed than Elizabeth had ever seen him.

"I never meant for you to learn about my involvement. I worried then that you might develop some mistaken feelings of gratitude towards me for saving your family's reputation. Gratitude is the last thing I would want from you. All I have ever desired—what I long for and crave with every fibre of my being—is that one day you would love me as fiercely and constantly as I love you."

His words nearly overwhelmed her, such was her joy at hearing him express what she had long feared he might never utter again. Before she could reassure him, he continued, pacing back and forth as his thoughts tumbled out.

"The more I pondered matters after the deed was done, I could not help but feel that I had erred. How could you ever be happy to count such a man as your brother?"

She endeavoured to stop his outpouring of self-reproach, but he anticipated her. "No, do not attempt to deny it! I can see how you have suffered his unwelcome attentions. I should have found a better way! Surely, there must have been someone else who could have been found to marry your sister—an honourable man who would not plague your family for all of your days."

Stopping him at last, Elizabeth interjected, "For someone so commonly described as reticent, you certainly have much to say this morning. I have something I would tell you, before my courage fails me, and I would beg you not to interrupt."

He nodded briefly, though his expression seemed similar to a condemned man facing the gallows.

"Would you like to know what my first thought was when you quit the inn at Lambton?" Elizabeth asked, her question clearly taking him by surprise. "It was precisely at that moment I fully realised what my foolish behaviour at Hunsford had cost me. It had cost me you.

"I knew of your involvement in the whole sorry affair before you even arrived." Shock overran his features, but she continued before he could speak. "As Kitty mentioned, Lydia had already betrayed your presence at her wedding, so I wrote to my aunt Gardiner and begged her to tell me all. You are beyond doubt, the best man I have ever known. It was too much for me to believe that you could ever bring yourself to love me again when I carried the burden of a fallen sister, and once she was saved, even my vanity was insufficient to believe that you could bear being brother to Wickham, that you could join your family to one who had so cruelly injured your own. Pray forgive me, but I did not believe anyone could ever love me so well as that."

Tears slowly spilled down Elizabeth's cheeks as she continued, her heightened emotions nearly choking her. "And now...now you stand here claiming that all you have ever wished is for me to love you, and I do! I believe I always will."

At her words, Mr Darcy stepped forward to hold her in his embrace. "Elizabeth, my darling, please do not cry, for your tears are my undoing."

He continued to hold her, speaking soft words of love in her ear as she slowly calmed, relishing the feel of his arms around her.

Once her tears had abated and only small shuddering breaths remained, Mr Darcy whispered with fervency, "Marry me, dearest, loveliest Elizabeth! Say that you will be mine as I am yours."

Pulling back to give him a brilliant, watery smile, she nodded vigorously, crying anew as she said, "Yes! Yes a thousand times over! I love you so, Fitzwilliam!"

Her words produced the largest smile Elizabeth had ever seen on Mr Darcy's face, complete with a devastatingly handsome set of dimples. How wonderful his happiness became him! Leaning his forehead against hers, he cupped her cheeks and wiped the remaining tears from her eyes. What followed surprised even Elizabeth as Mr Darcy raised her in his arms and swung her in a circle, laughing out his joy. As he set her back on her feet, she snaked her arms about his neck, hugging him fiercely in her delight.

A cough was heard from behind them, startling them both. Once Elizabeth had released Mr Darcy, she turned in embarrassment, only to spot her dumbfounded father gaping at the pair of them. Clearly, he had witnessed more than Elizabeth would have wished.

Addressing Mr Darcy with surprise, her father said, "So, this is the answer you could not give? In love with my Lizzy, are you? No need to answer, for the evidence before me is quite plain and frankly unsettling!"

"Papa!" Elizabeth protested, though she could not keep a laugh from her scolding tone.

"Allow me to have my say. I had thought you might possess some feelings, an inclination perhaps, for my daughter, but I cannot say I expected this, Mr Darcy!"

Turning to Elizabeth, he continued. "I recall informing you of my resolution to pay closer attention to my family, my daughters in particular, and here I have missed a fact of some significance! The daughter I always believed I knew best is in love—and do not attempt to deny it, for I see it written upon your very face—and I knew absolutely nothing about it!" Looking back and forth between the couple, he asked, "I assume there is quite the tale to tell?"

"I assure you, sir, I shall tell you all you wish to know if it will gain your consent for Miss Elizabeth's hand in marriage." Offering his arm, Elizabeth grasped it as she smiled up at him, her eyes beaming with delight.

"You will grant your consent, surely?" Elizabeth turned to her father, content to share this happy moment.

"I would never deny you, Lizzy, for I begin to think I have the measure of your young man. I wager you will do exceedingly well together. Exceedingly well, indeed."

EPILOGUE

<hr>

As the carriage door closed behind him, Darcy leant back against the squabs and breathed out a deep sigh of relief.

"My poor Fitzwilliam! What a trying day you have had! First, you tied yourself to such an impertinent creature for all eternity, then were forced to be agreeable while maintaining a dashing smile. 'Tis a miracle you have not yet collapsed from the strain!"

Turning to face his darling wife of only a few hours, Darcy laughed. "Minx! I cannot tell you how elated I am to be permitted to stop that lovely, impertinent mouth!"

Kissing her soundly as the carriage made its way south through Meryton, Darcy believed himself to be the luckiest man in the world. As he shifted his attentions towards her graceful neck, Darcy peppered kisses in between his whispered words.

"Every tease you utter tests my very resolve, wife."

Flushed and smiling, Elizabeth replied in a delightfully breathy tone, "Perhaps I ought to move to the opposite bench, husband, lest we scandalise your driver with our behaviour."

"*Our* driver, Elizabeth, and I think I possess enough self-control to last the journey to London."

Kissing her chastely, Darcy pulled her against his side, wrapping his arm around her while playing with the newly acquired golden band on her left hand. Contented, he asked, "Were you pleased with the day, my love?"

"I cannot think how I could be more pleased! Jane and I always wished our husbands would be friends, but I do not believe we ever envisioned marrying in the same ceremony! I am so relieved that Mr Bingley finally came to the point."

It had come as a shock to Darcy as well that his impetuous friend had delayed asking for his angel's hand as long as he did. Though he supposed the matter of dispatching Miss Bingley back to London with a flea in her ear and the unappealing consolation that she would gain a connexion to the Darcys at last, did supersede any thoughts of romance for however brief a time.

Laughing, Darcy replied, "Did you know that he actually blamed his reticence on me? Apparently, I had so thoroughly shocked him with our engagement and the revelations about the Wickhams that he scarcely let me enjoy a full night's rest for a week entire!"

Elizabeth kissed his cheek before settling herself once again in his embrace. "Remind me to thank Colonel Fitzwilliam for his assistance in hurrying Lydia and her husband on to Newcastle."

"I already have. Your sister was clearly well enough to travel, though I know too well how far Wickham will go to avoid honest work."

"Well, at least they were not present to spoil the day," Elizabeth opined, stroking his waistcoat before regarding him with a mischievous smile. "I do not wish to think on the Wickhams any longer, Fitzwilliam. I simply wish to admire my new husband."

Smiling into her sparkling eyes, Darcy pulled her closer. "I believe I can assist you with your study, my love. For I shall be similarly engaged admiring my lovely new wife for quite some time to come."

The End

Forgotten Betrothal

CONFUSED AND CHASTENED following her cruel rejection of Mr Darcy's proposal, Elizabeth Bennet returns to her aunt's home in Gracechurch Street. Unable to find solace while pondering her terrible misjudgment of his character, she is overwhelmed with guilt for how she treated the puzzling gentleman from Derbyshire. Fitzwilliam Darcy has retreated to his London home after being spurned by the lady he loves, and after serious reflection has come to the realisation that he never deserved Elizabeth's good opinion.

A CHANCE ENCOUNTER WITH MR DARCY brings Elizabeth the opportunity to seek forgiveness, and possibly, a new start to their budding romance. But the introduction of a stranger into Elizabeth's life threatens to reveal old family secrets that have the potential to truly unravel her world and all that she holds dear.

ABOUT THE AUTHOR

LM Romano is, as Miss Bingley would say, "a great reader", though she still owns to taking delight in many things–like teaching history and entertaining her very rambunctious toddler. A Northern California native, she currently lives with her husband and their adorable daughter in Ontario, California. She plans to continue writing, teaching, and reading countless books to her heart's content.